A Rude Awakening

Sleep stole over Longarm . . .

Some time later he roused from that slumber. All he heard was the howling of the wind and Pete Quinn snoring as loud as ever. Louder, in fact. And closer. Too close.

Longarm's eyes snapped open. The glow from the stove was just enough to show a dark figure looming over him. The old prospector was awake but still snoring so Longarm wouldn't wake up.

A rustle of clothing warned Longarm to roll to the side. The snoring stopped as Quinn grunted with effort. Something hit the floor with a loud *thunk*! An ax had landed where Longarm's head had been a second earlier. The ax was embedded in the floorboard. Quinn cursed as he wrenched the weapon free.

Longarm kicked upward and buried the heel of his boot in Quinn's ample belly. The prospector groaned and doubled over. Hurt but enraged, he finally got the ax free and slashed at Longarm, who rolled again to avoid the blow. When he came up, he had the Colt in his hand.

"Damn it, drop that ax, Quinn! I'll shoot!"

Quinn lunged at him. The ax whistled through the air again. Longarm pulled the trigger. Flame geysered from the Colt's muzzle. The bullet struck Quinn and flung him backward, but the ax was already flying straight at Longarm . . .

TABOR EVANS

LONGARM

AND THE PINE BOX PAYOFF

JOVE BOOKS, NEW YORK

THE BERKLEY PUBLISHING GROUP
Published by the Penguin Group
Penguin Group (USA) Inc.
375 Hudson Street, New York, New York 10014, USA
Penguin Group (Canada), 90 Eglinton Avenue East, Suite 700, Toronto, Ontario M4P 2Y3, Canada
(a division of Pearson Penguin Canada Inc.)
Penguin Books Ltd., 80 Strand, London WC2R 0RL, England
Penguin Group Ireland, 25 St. Stephen's Green, Dublin 2, Ireland (a division of Penguin Books Ltd.)
Penguin Group (Australia), 250 Camberwell Road, Camberwell, Victoria 3124, Australia
(a division of Pearson Australia Group Pty. Ltd.)
Penguin Books India Pvt. Ltd., 11 Community Centre, Panchsheel Park, New Delhi—110 017, India
Penguin Group (NZ), 67 Apollo Drive, Rosedale, North Shore 0632, New Zealand
(a division of Pearson New Zealand Ltd.)
Penguin Books (South Africa) (Pty.) Ltd., 24 Sturdee Avenue, Rosebank, Johannesburg 2196,
South Africa

Penguin Books Ltd., Registered Offices: 80 Strand, London WC2R 0RL, England

This is a work of fiction. Names, characters, places, and incidents either are the product of the author's imagination or are used fictitiously, and any resemblance to actual persons, living or dead, business establishments, events, or locales is entirely coincidental.

LONGARM AND THE PINE BOX PAYOFF

A Jove Book / published by arrangement with the author

PRINTING HISTORY
Jove edition / March 2008

Copyright © 2008 by The Berkley Publishing Group.
Cover illustration by Miro Sinovcic.

ISBN: 978-0-515-14425-3

JOVE®
Jove Books are published by The Berkley Publishing Group,
a division of Penguin Group (USA) Inc.,
375 Hudson Street, New York, New York 10014.
JOVE is a registered trademark of Penguin Group (USA) Inc.
The "J" design is a trademark belonging to Penguin Group (USA) Inc.

PRINTED IN THE UNITED STATES OF AMERICA

10 9 8 7 6 5 4 3 2 1

Chapter 1

The icy wind battered Longarm in the face, cold enough to sear his lungs and take his breath away. Thick swirls of snow filled the air. He couldn't see more than a few feet ahead of him. He squinted and made out a faint yellow glow, a blob of illumination coming from a window. As he staggered toward it, fighting the frigid wind, he ran into the wall of a building and bounced off. The impact almost made him fall.

He caught his balance and tried to pull his head down deeper into the sheepskin coat he wore. With one hand keeping his flat-crowned, snuff-brown Stetson in place and the other hand inside his coat clutching the butt of a Colt .45, he started forward again.

The wind carried the sound of a woman's scream to his ears.

Longarm bit back a curse and increased his speed to a trot. That was dangerous because he couldn't see very far and might run into something else. But he couldn't just stumble around and do nothing while Nicole was in danger. The scream came again and he steered toward it through the blizzard.

"Hey!"

1

The shout came from his right. Longarm twisted toward it. He didn't recognize the voice, didn't know if it belonged to friend or foe.

"Here he is! The bastard's over here!"

Foe, then.

Longarm dived aside as twin plumes of fire spouted from the barrels of a shotgun with a dull roar. He landed in a snowdrift next to a building. The stuff clogged his nose and eyes. He came up sputtering. His revolver hand was out of his coat now. The Colt bucked against his palm as he aimed at the spot where the Greener had gone off.

Longarm fired twice and heard a man howl in pain. He didn't know who he had just shot but he hoped he'd killed the son of a bitch. He lunged to his feet, practically swimming through the snow to do so.

More men shouted from somewhere nearby. Longarm felt his way along the wall of the building and came to the front of it, where a porch was built. Longarm dived into the opening under the structure and crawled for several yards.

It wasn't too bad under there. An improvement, actually. Some snow had blown underneath the porch and the wind whipped through as well, but not as strong as outside. Longarm pawed melted snow out of his eyes and looked around.

Clomping footsteps told him that one of the searchers was right beside the porch. He looked in that direction and was able to make out the dark columns of the man's legs against the lighter backdrop of the snow.

"Where the hell did he go? I thought he was right over here somewhere!"

"He didn't come this way!" A fainter voice, farther away.

Longarm wormed toward the edge of the porch. When he got there, he set the Colt down, reached out, and grabbed the man's ankles, toppling the searcher with a hard, unexpected heave. The man crashed to the ground with a startled yell.

2

Longarm grabbed the Colt and scrambled out. The gun rose and fell, thudded against something soft. The searcher stopped yelling, groaned, and lay still. Longarm felt around in the snow and found the shotgun that the man had dropped.

Whittle 'em down one by one. It would take a long time and a lot of luck, but it might work.

Longarm didn't have the time. Nicole screamed again. What the hell were they doing to her, anyway?

He jammed the Colt back in its holster, a cross-draw rig on his left hip. Clutched the scattergun and broke into a shambling run through the snow. Not everybody in this settlement was one of his enemies, but for now he had to assume that anybody he ran into wanted to kill him. The good folks were likely hunkered down somewhere, waiting for the killing to be over.

"Ace? Spike? Where the hell are you?"

Neither man answered. Longarm hoped they were both dead.

A long open space told him he was crossing the street. The undertaking parlor was on the other side. That was where they'd have Nicole.

The lion's den, like with Daniel in the Good Book.

A little ramshackle church back in West "by God" Virginia—Longarm had heard the story there first as a boy. Never understood how a fella could just walk right into a den full of lions without bein' scared enough to piss his pants.

Over time he had learned: Sometimes you didn't have any choice. The lions waited for you and you had to face them.

Like now.

Nicole screamed again, close this time. Right in front of him.

Longarm roared and charged forward. Sounded a mite like a lion himself, if he'd stopped to think about it. He

3

didn't. The swirling snow cleared for a second and he saw the boardwalk in front of the undertaking parlor. He bounded onto it, hit the door with his shoulder.

He couldn't just charge in shooting. Too great a chance he'd hit Nicole or some other innocent. So he went to the floor as soon as he was inside. A six-gun blasted. Longarm rolled, came up on a knee, and saw the man tracking the revolver barrel toward him. Longarm triggered one of the Greener's barrels.

The buckshot slammed into the gunman and threw him backward like a rag doll. He hit an empty coffin sitting on a pair of sawhorses and knocked it off. The man landed on the coffin and busted the side of it. He lay there in the debris and didn't move. The charge from the shotgun had shredded his chest.

Longarm's ears still echoed from the blast but he heard feet scuffling anyway. He swung the scattergun in that direction but held off on the trigger as he saw Roland backing away. The man had one arm looped around Nicole's neck. The other hand held a pistol, which he pressed to her side.

"I'll kill her, Marshal. I swear I will."

Longarm didn't doubt it. Vance Roland was not only one of the ugliest bastards Longarm had ever seen, he was a cold-blooded murderer, too.

"Take it easy, Roland. It's over. No need to make things any worse."

Roland smiled, which just made him uglier. "How can it get any worse than it already is?"

He had a point there. A man could only hang once.

But there were other ways of dying.

"Hurt her and I'll see to it that you're praying for a hang rope before you cross the divide."

"You wouldn't do that. You're a lawman."

"I've been known to disremember that from time to time, old son."

Something flickered in Roland's watery blue eyes. Fear? Surrender?

Hope.

"Shit!"

Longarm started to come up and around. The wind howled through the open door, covered the sound of footsteps until it was too late. Something crashed down on Longarm's head, drove him to the floor. The shotgun slipped out of his fingers.

A booted foot slammed into his back, pinned him to the planks. Roland laughed from across the room.

"Now we'll see who's going to be praying for death."

Chapter 2

Billy Vail pushed some papers across his desk. He was bald and pink and looked more like somebody's kindly old grandpa than a lawman.

"This one's a woman."

"I know what a woman is, Billy." Longarm took a puff on his cheroot and blew a smoke ring toward the banjo clock on the wall of the chief marshal's office. He reached for the reports. "I've met up with one or two in my life."

"Not any as slick as this one is."

Longarm frowned, thought back, shook his head.

"I wouldn't say that, neither."

"You know what I mean. Just read the damn reports."

Longarm read. Half a dozen reports told the same story but with different players and locations from Texas to California. An attractive young woman made the acquaintance of a wealthy older man. After a while the woman was gone and so was a healthy chunk of the man's money.

"I reckon Nancy Gilworth, Nell Gray, Nora Graham, and these other gals are all the same woman?"

"That's what we figure. Pretty much the same thing happens every time."

Longarm tossed the reports back on Vail's desk. "I don't

see how some petty swindling concerns the Justice Department, Billy."

"Read that last one again and pay particular attention to the name of the fella who got swindled."

Longarm sorted out the stack of papers, found the right one. He let out a low whistle of surprise.

"Yeah, I didn't notice that the first time through. Congressman, ain't he?"

"Yeah, and he's damned upset about getting taken that way." Vail shrugged. "But I reckon his feelings are hurt, too. He thought the girl really cared about him."

"So he's kicked up enough of a fuss in Washington that the muckety-mucks in the Justice Department agreed to look for her."

Vail nodded. "Meaning that they'll have us look for her, which means that I'm telling you to find her. Last place she was seen was on a train headed for Virginia City."

"How long ago was that?"

"Two weeks."

Longarm shook his head. "You don't reckon she's still there, do you? Shoot, Billy, she could be 'most anywhere by now."

"You have to pick up the trail somewhere. Virginia City's as good a place as any."

The case didn't seem promising to Longarm. Seemed like a waste of his time and the government's money, in fact. But since he was a deputy United States marshal and Vail was the chief marshal for the Western District, Longarm figured he would do the best he could to find the woman.

"Get your travel vouchers from Henry. Don't waste any time on this one, Custis. We're under considerable pressure."

"I never knew you to be one to worry overmuch about such things, Billy."

Vail pushed his glasses up on his nose. His eyes burned

like those of the hard-riding Texas Ranger he had once been.

"I hate politics with a passion but sometimes you've got to pay attention. That congressman's on the committee that holds the purse strings. And it's damned near time for a new budget."

Longarm couldn't argue with that. He clamped his teeth down on the three-for-a-nickel cheroot, came to his feet.

"I'll do my best, Billy."

"I know you will. You always have."

Longarm left the inner office. Henry, the four-eyed young fella who played the typewriter in the outer office, handed him a stack of travel vouchers.

"Try not to exceed the allotted amount this time, Marshal Long. And remember to keep your receipts for any additional expenses."

Longarm perched a hip on the corner of Henry's desk, blew smoke sort of careless-like in his direction.

"You ever get tired of adding up numbers, Henry?"

"Not at all. I find them fascinating. And I enjoy their consistency. They never change, unlike people."

Longarm shook his head. "Sounds mighty boring to me, something that never changes like that."

"Obviously, our minds work in different ways."

Longarm's cheroot had gone out. He fished a lucifer out of his vest pocket, snapped it into life with his thumbnail, and set fire to the gasper once again.

"I reckon they do, at that. And there ain't hardly a day goes by I don't thank the Good Lord that's true."

Henry scowled. He was good at it.

Longarm tucked the vouchers into an inside pocket in the jacket of his brown tweed suit. He also wore high-topped black boots, a boiled white shirt, and a string tie. A watch chain looped across from one pocket of his vest to the other. A heavy turnip watch was attached to one end of the chain. Welded to the other end was a two-shot .41-caliber derringer

9

that had saved Longarm's bacon more times than he could count. A Colt .45 rode in a cross-draw rig on his left hip. He was the very picture of a modern frontier lawman. The sort of gent Uncle Sam could be proud of.

Even if Henry didn't much like him.

Longarm left the office with a wave, walked out of Denver's Federal Building, and headed for his rented room on the other side of Cherry Creek, near the place where gold had been discovered some twenty years earlier. The sky was overcast and a chilly wind tugged at Longarm's hat. Winter was coming on.

He was almost back to the boardinghouse when he spotted the hombre following him. Tall drink of water, almost as tall as Longarm himself. Dressed in range clothes. A battered old hat with a tight-curled brim pulled low over a hawklike face.

The butt of a revolver with well-worn walnut grips jutted up from a holster on the man's hip. His hand hovered too close to it for comfort.

Longarm had never seen the man before but that didn't mean anything. He had plenty of enemies he'd never met, relatives of men he had sent to prison or killed in the line of duty. So he wasn't surprised to hear the harsh yell.

"Long! Custis Long!"

The man clawed at his gun as the words came out of his mouth. Turning, Longarm saw the motion from the corner of his eye. He didn't waste any time making his own draw. His hand swept across his body, palmed the .45 from the holster, brought it level.

Flame geysered from the muzzle a split second before the other man's gun erupted. The would-be killer's shot went wild because the slug from Longarm's gun had already buried itself in the man's chest and knocked him back a step. Not too wild, though. Longarm heard the bullet lash the air close by his head.

The man went over backward and landed with his arms

and legs splayed out. The gun thudded to the ground beside him. Not many pedestrians were on the street because of the cold, blustery weather. The stray bullet had hit the brick wall of a building and done no harm. Somebody ran to fetch the police anyway.

Longarm walked over, kicked the gun out of reach, looked down at the dying man. The man gasped for breath he couldn't seem to get. Air wheezed through the hole in his chest.

"You don't have much time, old son. Who are you? Why'd you throw down on me?"

"Ch-Chet Bowles . . ."

"You ain't Chet Bowles. He was hanged six months ago."

"M-my b-brother . . ."

"Oh. Figured to settle the score because I'm the one who brung him in, eh?"

"You b-bastard!"

Longarm shifted the cheroot to the other side of his mouth, spoke around it. "I been called a lot worse."

Chet Bowles's brother wheezed again, heaved a long sigh. His staring eyes began to glaze over in death. Longarm shook his head and punched the empty shell out of the Colt's cylinder and replaced it with a fresh cartridge. A gloomy, overcast day like this, some folks would say it was a good day for dying.

Longarm disagreed and figured that Chet Bowles's brother would have, too.

There was no such thing.

Chapter 3

Later that afternoon Longarm caught a northbound train for Cheyenne, Wyoming. A couple of blue-uniformed Denver policemen had questioned him about the shooting but hadn't detained him. Once they saw that the survivor of the fracas was Deputy U.S. Marshal Custis Long, they pretty much knew what to expect. This was hardly the first time some varmint with a grudge had gone gunning for the big federal lawman.

When the train reached Cheyenne that evening, Longarm transferred to a westbound. Snow flurries danced in the air on the station platform. The first real storm of the winter hadn't hit yet. Longarm hoped it would hold off until the case was over and he was back in Denver.

This Union Pacific train would take him to Salt Lake City. He wouldn't stay there long, just long enough to switch over to a Southern Pacific train that would carry him the rest of the way to Virginia City, Nevada.

Longarm didn't care all that much for Salt Lake City. Most Mormons were all right, but he had gotten crosswise with the Avenging Angels a time or two in the past. Once they had even abandoned him in the desert to die a slow death. He would have, too, if he hadn't managed to build himself a makeshift wind wagon.

Some of those Saints had long memories. He didn't want to run into any trouble that would keep him from the assignment Billy Vail had given him.

So he didn't leave the depot in Salt Lake City even though he had to wait a couple of hours the next morning before the Southern Pacific train pulled out. It wasn't snowing at all there, but the weather was cold enough that Longarm camped out next to a pot-bellied stove until it was time to go, and was grateful for its warmth.

From Utah on through the passes into Nevada, then over the mountains into the valley of the Humboldt River. Longarm had been on the Humboldt numerous times. The valley was actually a broad basin, ugly and severe in its arid barrenness. Longarm didn't cotton to it at all. He was glad when the tracks reached the mountains again and curved down the western side of a rugged range through the Washoe Valley toward the old mining town of Virginia City.

Five years earlier in 1875 fire had destroyed quite a bit of the settlement. That wasn't the first time a conflagration threatened to wipe out Virginia City. Each time the citizens had rebuilt the town. The aftermath of the blaze of '75 was no different. Virginia City came back bigger and better than ever.

Longarm traveled light when he was on assignment. He had only his McClellan saddle, Winchester, and a small war bag with him. He turned down the offer of help from a porter and carried the gear himself from the train station to the International Hotel, a five-story brick-and-mortar edifice that had replaced an earlier, smaller hotel of the same name destroyed in the latest fire.

Virginia City was the center of the great Comstock Lode mining empire. Great cattle ranches sprawled over the wooded hills and valleys, too. So with wealth above the ground and wealth below, all sorts of people came to Virginia City. The clerk on duty at the International Hotel didn't bat an eyelash when Longarm placed his saddle on the fancy parquet floor and laid the Winchester on the desk.

"Need a room."

"Yes, sir." The clerk turned the register around. "If you'll just sign in . . ."

Longarm plucked a pen from an inkwell on the desk and scrawled *Custis Parker, Albuquerque* in the book. He wasn't from Albuquerque, of course, but Parker really was his middle name and he often used it as an alias when working undercover. He didn't have any real reason to do that here. Old habits were just hard to break.

"Thank you, Mr. Parker. Would you like us to take care of your rifle and saddle for you?"

"You can store the saddle but I'll keep the rifle with me."

"Whatever you like." The clerk took a key off the pegboard behind him. "Room Four Eleven." He rang a bell on the desk with a sharp blow from the heel of his hand. "Boy!"

The "boy" who answered the summons was probably fifty years old and hobbled like a stove-up cowhand. He reached for Longarm's war bag and rifle. Longarm let him take the bag but picked up the Winchester himself.

The clerk handed the key to the bellboy. "Four eleven, Calvin."

"Yes, sir." Calvin limped away with Longarm following. "Right over here to the elevator, sir."

Longarm had been in elevators before. He didn't much like them. The idea of a little room moving up and down between floors of a building just didn't seem right to him. But he didn't much want to climb four flights of stairs, either, so he got in and let an operator who wore the same sort of uniform as Calvin ring a bell and move a lever back and forth and send the elevator rising through the bowels of the hotel with the rumble of hydraulics.

The International Hotel was a fancy place all the way

around. Expensive, too. Henry would likely complain about that when Longarm got back to Denver.

But the woman known variously as Nancy Gilworth, Nell Gray, and Nora Graham had expensive tastes. Especially in men. If she had come to Virginia City to carry out the same sort of swindle as she had in other places, the International was where she would stay to find the most suitable targets.

As the elevator ground upward, Longarm looked at Calvin and the uniformed operator and decided he might as well get started. "I believe a friend of mine stayed here a couple of weeks ago. She might even still be here. Really nice-looking woman, about twenty-five years old with blonde hair and blue eyes."

That was the description Longarm had taken from the reports he'd read in Billy Vail's office. Sort of vague but the only thing he had to go by.

Calvin looked back over his shoulder. "What's the lady's name, sir?"

Now that was a problem. Longarm knew all her aliases but not the name she would be using now. He recalled the one on the most recent report and threw it out there as a long shot.

"Nora Graham."

Calvin shook his head. So did the elevator operator. The name meant nothing to them. Longarm had expected as much. And the description was too sketchy to do any good.

It had been worth a try. The elevator lurched to a halt. Longarm wondered if any of these contraptions ever busted and fell down their shaft. He wouldn't want to be inside one if that ever happened.

Calvin led him down a thickly carpeted hallway to Room 411, unlocked the door, and ushered him into a sumptuously furnished room. Yeah, Henry was gonna have a fit at the cost of these accommodations. Calvin put the rifle on the big four-poster bed, then opened the curtains over the large single window.

Longarm pressed a coin into the gnarled old hand and made one more try. "You've done some cowboyin' in your time, I reckon."

Calvin's eyes lit up. "I rode for spreads in Texas and Colorado. You ever work cattle, Mr. Parker?"

"Did quite a bit of it when I first came out here after the Late Unpleasantness. Swallowed a heap of dust riding drag up the Chisholm Trail on a few drives."

Calvin slapped his thigh and chortled. "Yeah, I been up that trail a lot of times myself. Drove the chuck wagon the last few times after my damn horse took a spill while we were tryin' to head off a stampede. Wrecked my knee when the critter fell on it, so I couldn't ride no more."

"If there was a stampede going on, you're lucky you didn't get trampled into the ground."

Calvin laughed again. "Tell me about it! My poor, sinful life sure flashed before my eyes right about then, I do declare!" Now that a connection had been established between him and Longarm, a thoughtful look came over his wizened face. "Say, that gal you were askin' about . . . is she really a friend of yours?"

Longarm sighed. "She was . . . until she up and ran off. We were even engaged." He sighed again, more dramatically this time. "She always talked about coming to Virginia City. I thought I might find her here and convince her to take me back."

"Why'd she leave?"

"I, uh, strayed." Longarm looked at the carpet like he was too embarrassed to meet the old-timer's eyes.

"You oughta be ashamed o' yourself."

"I am, I swear I am. That's why I want to make it right with her." An idea occurred to Longarm. He recalled that when he signed the registration book downstairs, it was turned to the very first page. "What happens to the old registration books after they're full?"

"Why, they keep 'em in Mr. Prentice's office. He's the manager of the hotel."

"You know, it's possible sweet Nora might be using a different name. But I'd sure recognize her handwriting, so if I could get a look at the registrations from the past two weeks, I'd know if she's been here."

Calvin looked doubtful, scratched at his lantern jaw. "I reckon I could get the last book from the office, but I ain't supposed to mess with things like that. Might get me in trouble. I need this job, mister."

Longarm took out a gold double eagle and held it where Calvin could see it. "This make it worth your while?"

The coin disappeared with the speed of a striking snake. "I can slip it up here to you tonight, but it'll have to be pretty late. The clerk dozes most of the time after midnight."

"That'll do just fine. I'm much obliged to you, Calvin."

"You can have a look through the book, but then you gotta give it back so I can put it back in the office."

Longarm nodded. "No problem." He had no idea what the handwriting of his quarry looked like, but she had a habit, too: using the initials N.G. whenever she picked a new false name. If a single woman with those initials had checked into the International within the past two weeks, there was a good chance she was the one Longarm was looking for. If that woman matched the description, then the odds were even better.

Just knowing for sure that she had been here and knowing the alias she was using would be a good first step in finding her.

Calvin scuttled toward the door. "All right. I'll be back." He hesitated on his way out. "You won't tell nobody I'm helpin' you?"

"Not a soul, partner."

It had probably been a long time since anybody had referred to Calvin by that term. He grinned as he went out and shut the door.

Longarm stretched out on the bed to smoke a cheroot. The bet might not pay off, but at least he had dealt out the first cards in this hand.

Chapter 4

Longarm didn't leave the hotel that evening. He ate dinner in the hotel dining room, had a couple of shots of Maryland rye in the barroom off the lobby. A friendly, low-stakes poker game provided a couple of hours of pleasant diversion. Then he went back upstairs to wait for Calvin to deliver the registration book.

The old cowhand-turned-bellboy arrived at 12:27 by Longarm's turnip watch. He announced his presence with a soft, stealthy knock on the door. Longarm asked who it was, then moved a step to one side just in case somebody in the hall took a shot through the door. Those old habits again.

"Calvin. I got what you wanted, Mr. Parker."

Longarm opened the door. The old-timer shuffled in. Clutched in his gnarled hands was a thin, leather-bound book, which he held out to Longarm.

"Make it quick if you would, sir, so's I can put it back 'fore anybody notices it's gone."

Longarm flipped back two weeks in the register and started running his finger down the list of names signed there. It didn't take him long to find Miss Nicole Gardner, allegedly from St. Louis.

"There she is. Has to be her."

Calvin craned his neck. "Lemme see . . . Oh, yeah, I recollect that lady. Young and blonde and mighty pretty, just like you said, Mr. Parker." His eyes widened as he remembered something else. "Oh, shoot."

"What is it?"

"You said you and the gal was supposed to get hitched?"

"That's right."

"Well, I pure-dee hate to tell you this, Mr. Parker, but I'm afraid the lady callin' herself Miss Gardner has already found herself another beau."

Longarm tried to look suitably concerned instead of excited that the trail had started to heat up. "You know that for a fact, do you?"

"I'm afraid so. She met up with Mr. Harvey Kellogg right here in the hotel, when there was a banquet one night for some businessmen visitin' from back East. He started courtin' her right off. I took him up to her room a couple o' times myself, and he always had a bouquet o' fresh flowers with him."

Longarm frowned. "Fresh flowers? At this time of year?"

"When you've got as much money as Mr. Kellogg, I reckon things like the seasons don't really matter as much."

Longarm ran a thumbnail along the line of his jaw. "Rich hombre, is he?"

"Damn right."

"Mine owner?"

"No, he owns one of the banks where them minin' magnets keep *their* money."

Longarm didn't bother telling the old-timer that it was *magnates*, not magnets. Anyway, those fellas attracted money like it was iron filings and they were lodestones, so the description wasn't that far off.

"So she's still here in town, still being courted by this Kellogg hombre? Still staying here in the hotel?"

Calvin looked uncomfortable. "Wellll . . . Miss Gardner's done moved out of the hotel. I think . . . uh, I think she's stayin' at Mr. Kellogg's house."

"How old is Kellogg?"

"Fifty if he's a day. But still handsome and distinguished-like, you know, the way rich fellas are."

Longarm's expression was suitably grim as he nodded. "Yeah, I know." He snapped the registration book closed and handed it back to Calvin. "Where does he live?"

"Oh, I hadn't ought to tell you that, Mr. Parker. You don't want to go over there and cause a ruckus. You'll get hurt."

"Kellogg a tough hombre, is he?"

"Not so's you'd notice, but the bodyguards who work for him are."

It was no surprise that a rich banker would hire men to protect him. But they would step aside from the badge of a deputy United States marshal. Especially when Harvey Kellogg found out that Miss Nicole Gardner had a long history of swindling rich older gents just like him.

"I won't cause any trouble, Calvin. And don't worry, nobody will ever know that you had anything to do with this. I'll keep you out of it."

"I'd be much obliged for that, Mr. Parker. It ain't easy for a stove-up ol' cuss like me to get work."

Longarm patted the old-timer on the shoulder and slipped him another coin, a five-dollar gold piece this time. "Now, where does Kellogg live?"

Calvin sighed. "Over on B Street, four blocks back up the hill. You can't miss it. It's the biggest house on the block. Got a bunch o' them gables and balustrades and such-like. Looks like it ought to be back in Chicago or New York or some place like that instead of here in Virginia City."

"All right. I really am obliged to you, Calvin."

"What're you gonna do?"

"I don't rightly know yet. I'll have to think on it."

23

That wasn't strictly true. Longarm had already made up his mind what he was going to do. As soon as Calvin was gone, he was heading right over to Harvey Kellogg's house, where he would arrest the woman calling herself Nicole Gardner. He would take her to the local hoosegow, show his badge and bona fides to the sheriff, and lock Miss Gardner up until he could board the next eastbound train with her. This case would be wrapped up in a hurry.

Sometimes you got lucky that way. Longarm would take all the luck he could get.

Calvin hobbled out of the room. Longarm closed the door and waited a few minutes before leaving. The International Hotel had a set of rear stairs. He went down them instead of taking the elevator.

Virginia City had a hundred saloons and four churches. That ratio was just about right for a mining boomtown. Unlike some settlements where the boardwalks might as well be rolled up at sundown, Virginia City never completely closed up shop. Because of that a lot of people were still on the streets as Longarm walked toward the house where Harvey Kellogg lived.

The town was built on the side of a mountain, so most of the streets sloped either up or down. Kellogg's mansion was up B Street. Longarm counted the blocks until he was sure he was in the right one. As Calvin had said, it was hard to miss the Kellogg house. It was the largest one on the block, a gabled, turreted monstrosity set behind a white-washed wrought-iron fence and a good-sized lawn dotted with shrubbery.

Lights burned in several of the windows despite the late hour. That was good. Longarm wouldn't have to rouse the whole household when he arrested Nicole Gardner. They were already awake.

He unlatched the gate in the fence, swung it back. The hinges squealed. Kellogg ought to speak to his caretaker

24

about that. A flagstone walk led to the large porch built onto the front of the house.

Longarm was halfway up that walk when two shots suddenly roared from inside the mansion.

Chapter 5

He stopped short and stood there for a second. He wasn't sure he had actually heard what he thought he'd heard.

Then another sharp report sounded inside the house. Yep, definitely a gunshot.

Followed by a scream.

Longarm broke into a run. He didn't know what was going on in there but he intended to find out.

He dashed up the walk and took the steps to the porch in one bound. His gun was in his hand without really having to think about drawing it. He tried the front door. Locked. Hit it with his shoulder but it was too heavy and thick to spring it open that way.

Another shot roared and a window shattered at the corner of the house. Longarm could reach the window from the porch so he raced down to it and peered in through the curtain, which had been knocked askew.

A man and woman struggled in what appeared to be a library or study. Shelves of dark, leather-bound volumes lined the walls. The couple turned and Longarm saw the woman's face. Young, attractive, framed by thick wings of pale blonde hair.

Nicole Gardner, or Longarm missed his guess.

But the man she struggled with wasn't Harvey Kellogg. He was too young to be the banker. Calvin had said Kellogg was around fifty. This man was no more than thirty, with short, sandy hair and spectacles. Wearing a dressing gown. Slender enough so that he couldn't overpower the woman without a considerable struggle.

And she was giving him one, sure as shooting.

Longarm looked for the gun. It was in the woman's hand. Behind her was a desk. Slumped at the desk was a man with thinning gray hair. Blood pooled under his head. The back of his skull was a mess where a bullet or two had exploded out of it.

That would be Harvey Kellogg, Longarm supposed.

The man in the dressing gown had one hand on the wrist of the woman's gun hand. His other arm was around her as they grappled. She reached back with her free hand, plucked some sort of heavy paperweight off the desk, slammed it into the side of the man's head. He let go of her wrist and slumped to the floor. She swung the gun toward him.

Longarm kicked out the broken window and thrust the Colt through the opening. "Hold it! Drop that gun!"

The barrel jerked toward him and geysered flame. The slug hit the side of the window and chewed splinters out of the frame. Longarm ducked and grimaced as the slivers of wood stung his face.

In that split second the woman spun and darted out the open door of the study.

Longarm might have been able to snap a shot at her and bring her down as she fled. He had gunned down women in the past when they were trying their damnedest to kill him. But for some reason he held his fire. He didn't know for certain exactly what was going on here even though it seemed pretty obvious.

Instead he turned and long-legged it back down the porch toward the door. When he got there, he didn't hesitate. He blasted two shots into the lock and then drove the heel of his boot against the wood just below the knob.

The door flew open with a rending crash.

The sandy-haired man appeared to be all right, just stunned. And the unlucky hombre slumped at the desk was already as dead as he was ever going to be. So Longarm followed the patter of running footsteps and went after the woman.

She was headed for the rear of the house. Longarm didn't know the mansion's layout. That slowed him down. He cursed under his breath as he ran down a corridor that came to an end at a blank wall. That meant he had to retrace his steps and lose valuable time.

The rear door was blowing and banging in the cold wind when he got there. That open door made him a target as he went through it, so he moved as fast as he could. He ducked into the darkness of a garden, skidded to a stop, listened for sounds of escape.

Another door slammed somewhere on the far side of the garden. Longarm headed toward the sound. Might be a trap or a decoy, but he had to take that chance. He had to capture Nicole Gardner.

She had moved right past swindling to murder.

The dark bulk of a carriage house and stable loomed beyond the garden. Longarm wasn't surprised; a mansion such as Kellogg's nearly always had such outbuildings.

He slowed to a trot as he neared the carriage house. The woman was either in there or in the stable.

The stable was the better bet. If she knew how to ride, she could take one of the horses and get away. Longarm edged in that direction.

He was nearly at the stable doors when they burst open and a horse lunged out into the night. Longarm threw himself to the side to keep from getting trampled. He caught a glimpse of the woman leaning forward over the horse's neck as she urged it into a gallop.

She was riding bareback and astride. Pale calves and thighs flashed in the moonlight.

Longarm hit the ground, rolled over. Instinct pulled him around and brought the Colt up. Again something stopped him from firing. He told himself that he would be shooting blind because of the bad light. Too much danger of stray bullets hitting an innocent person.

He sprang up, ran a few steps, stopped, and muttered, "Damn it!" He couldn't catch Nicole Gardner on foot. Not with her mounted and evidently a pretty good rider. And he didn't have another horse handy.

Unless there was one in the stable.

Longarm whirled and ran into the building. It was dark, so he took a lucifer from his vest pocket and lit it with a snap of his fingernail. The glare from the sulfur match revealed several horses in stalls. Longarm lit a lantern he saw hanging on a nail driven into a post. Then he grabbed a halter from a pegboard where tack was hanging and opened one of the stall doors.

The horse inside the stall was a leggy chestnut. It shied away but calmed down quickly when Longarm spoke to it in a soft voice. He got the halter on the horse as quickly as he could. The woman was getting farther away with each passing second.

Longarm didn't take the time to find a saddle. He could ride bareback, too. That was the way he'd learned as a kid back in West "by God" Virginia.

He swung up onto the horse and banged his heels against its flanks. The horse lunged out of the stable and onto a dirt path that looped around the garden and the house. Longarm guessed that it led back to B Street. That was the way the fleeing Nicole Gardner had gone.

Halfway around the house somebody jumped in front of the horse. Longarm hauled back on the reins, shouted, "Whoa, damn it, whoa!"

The horse almost ran over the crazy son of a bitch despite that. The figure flung itself backward, stumbled, fell.

"Help me! For God's sake, help me!"

The voice was a strangled croak. Longarm held the horse in, hesitated while he tried to figure out what to do. He heard the swiftly fading rataplan of hoofbeats as the blonde vanished into the night. She already had a good lead on him.

Probably too good for him to be able to catch her right away. He grimaced, sighed, shook his head. Slid down from the horse and leaned over the fallen figure.

"How bad are you hurt, old son?"

"You . . . you . . . who are you?"

Longarm grasped the man's arm, lifted him. "Don't worry about that. Just tell me how bad you're hurt."

He wasn't surprised that the man wore a dressing gown. This was the sandy-haired gent who'd been wrestling with Nicole Gardner.

The man lifted a hand to his head. A dark trail of blood wormed down his face from a gash in his scalp where the blonde had walloped him.

"I . . . I think I'm all right. I was just stunned when Miss Gardner hit me with that paperweight. You *are* the man who was at the window when we were struggling?"

"That's right."

"Who are you?"

"Custis Long. Deputy U.S. Marshal out of Denver."

"A lawman! Thank God!" The man clutched at Longarm's sleeve. "You have to go after her. Do you know what she's done?"

Longarm figured he already knew the answer but he wanted this fella to confirm it. "What?"

"She's murdered poor Mr. Kellogg! She killed him, that . . . that brazen hussy!"

31

Chapter 6

The sandy-haired hombre's name was Miles Ambrose. He was Harvey Kellogg's secretary, he explained as he led Longarm into the mansion.

"We should probably summon the Virginia City authorities."

"Let's eat the apple one bite at a time. Take me to the room where Kellogg got shot and tell me what happened."

Ambrose turned pale and looked away as he took Longarm into the book-lined study. Kellogg hadn't moved. Hadn't been moved, actually, since he wasn't ever going anywhere under his own power again.

"I was already asleep when a pair of shots woke me." Ambrose had to force the words out as he looked at everything else in the room except the corpse with the ruined skull. "I got up and ran downstairs to see what had happened."

"You live here?"

"Yes, I have my own room upstairs."

"Any other servants in the house?"

For a second Ambrose looked like he might take offense at being referred to as a servant. Then he shrugged it off.

"No, no one else lives here. The cook and the housekeeper and the caretaker just come during the day."

"What about a stableman?"

"The same man works as the caretaker for the estate. He handles both jobs."

Longarm nodded. "But the woman lives here?"

"Yes." Ambrose finally looked at Kellogg's body. His eyes revealed anger. "I cautioned Mr. Kellogg that he was making a mistake. It was not only highly improper to have an unmarried young woman under the same roof, it was also very unwise."

"He was courtin' her?"

"They were betrothed."

"Gonna get hitched, eh?" Longarm shook his head. "Not anymore."

"No." Ambrose had to choke out the word.

"If they were engaged, why would she up and shoot him?"

"I'm sure I have no idea. I've believed all along that Miss Gardner was simply after Mr. Kellogg's money and that she had no intention of ever really marrying him. Perhaps he discovered that and they quarreled over it."

Given the history of the woman who currently called herself Nicole Gardner, Longarm knew that was probably true. The swindling part, anyway.

"What happened after you heard the shots?"

"As I said, I ran down here from upstairs. I knew that Mr. Kellogg was in the habit of working in his study until the hour was quite late, so I came here first to make sure he was all right. It didn't actually occur to me that . . . that Miss Gardner might have shot him until I opened the door and saw her standing there with the gun in her hand."

"She'd already ventilated Kellogg?"

"Yes. He was . . . the way you see him now." Ambrose swallowed hard and looked a little sick.

"What did the woman do then?"

Ambrose's eyes widened at the memory. "She took a shot at me! She tried to kill me, too!"

That matched up with the shots Longarm had heard from outside. "So then you jumped her?"

"I . . . I suppose so. Everything is all jumbled up in my mind. But I knew that she had killed Mr. Kellogg and that if I didn't stop her, she would kill me, too. The gun went off again while we were struggling . . ." He glanced toward the window. "The shot broke the glass. Then she hit me with the paperweight and knocked me down. Then you were there, Marshal Long, shouting at her." Ambrose paused. "You saved my life."

"Too bad I didn't get here a spell sooner. Might've been able to save Kellogg's life, too."

Longarm stepped over to the desk, grasped the dead man's shoulders, lifted him so that he flopped back in the chair. Kellogg had been shot at close range. One bullet in the center of his forehead, the other in his right cheek just under the eye. Not much of his face was left.

Ambrose shuddered and turned away again.

An insistent pounding sounded in the house. It came from the direction of the front door. Longarm knew someone must have reported the shooting to the Virginia City police.

"Go let 'em in, Ambrose, and tell them everything you told me."

"Where are you going, Marshal?"

"After Miss Gardner. She's already got a big lead, but I'll see if I can pick up her trail."

"Be careful. She's already killed once tonight."

Longarm knew that. He didn't intend to let it happen again.

He went out the rear of the house. The horse's reins were tied to a tree in the side yard. Longarm mounted up and cantered back toward the center of Virginia City. Nicole Gardner had been headed in that direction when she fled. The boomtown was a busy place even this late, but Longarm figured the sight of a beautiful blonde woman galloping hell-bent-for-leather through the settlement, bareback and astride, was unusual enough to have been noticed.

It didn't take him long to find several people who had seen Nicole. They all agreed that she'd been headed south. Carson City, the state capital, was southwest. She might be headed there. Or she could be striking out into the more rugged country that was due south, a landscape of mountains and desert where the settlements were few and far between.

Or she might circle around and try to sneak back into Virginia City. She was a woman alone, on a stolen horse, with no supplies, no money, and only the gun she had used to kill a man.

Longarm thought the chances were good she'd come back.

The night was too dark to read sign. He would have to try to pick up Nicole's trail in the morning. He rode back to Harvey Kellogg's house. The place was lit up like Christmas now and crowded with police officers.

They acted a mite suspicious of Longarm when he showed up. His badge and bona fides identifying him as a deputy U.S. marshal took care of that. Miles Ambrose further explained that Longarm hadn't even been inside the house when Kellogg was killed.

A blustery, red-faced policeman assured Longarm that they would send wires all across the state, warning lawmen to keep an eye out for the blonde fugitive. "That's how modern law enforcement works, Marshal Long. The days of the lone manhunter are over."

Longarm didn't waste the time or energy to argue with the fella. Just nodded and said that he was much obliged. You never could tell, the telegrams might do some good. Some local star packer might spot Nicole Gardner, recognize her from her description, and arrest her.

But Longarm sure as hell wouldn't hold his breath waiting for that to happen.

36

He returned the horse to the stable. He would rent a mount the next morning and throw his own saddle on it. Some provisions, a couple of boxes of shells for his Winchester and the Colt, and he would be ready to take up Nicole's trail. He had tracked down plenty of owlhoots and killers during his years as a lawman. Despite what that full-of-himself police officer said, there was still a place on the frontier for a lone manhunter.

Or in this case, a lone woman hunter.

Chapter 7

Longarm rode out of Virginia City the next morning when
the sun was just peeking over the Stillwater Range to the
east. The brown tweed suit, the vest, and the string tie were
gone, packed away in his war bag. He was dressed for the
trail in denim trousers, a dark blue flannel shirt, and a
sheepskin coat to keep out the cold winds. The coat did a
fair job at that, but Longarm still felt a mite chilled.

His Winchester was snugged in a saddle sheath. The
saddlebags strapped over the back of the rented horse held
plenty of ammunition and enough food to last Longarm for
several days. He had two canteens full of water as well.
There were some dry stretches out there south of Virginia
City.

Every set of horseshoes left distinctive prints. As soon
as it was light enough to see, Longarm had gone to Kellogg's house and studied the tracks left in the dirt lane by
Nicole's mount as she fled. Once he had memorized the
various nicks in the iron, the way a couple of the nails had
been bent over funny by whoever had put them on, things
like that, he would know those prints wherever he saw
them from now on.

All he had to do was find them again. Not an easy task

considering how many people rode in and out of Virginia City every day.

But Longarm had the time to look. He had nothing but time, in fact, because he wouldn't be heading back to Denver until he had Nicole Gardner in custody.

He rode down C Street past the big two-story schoolhouse on the edge of town. Hills folded together to the south. Scattered through those hills were some of the mines that gave the Comstock Lode its wealth. At the end of C Street several trails branched off to those mines. Longarm figured Nicole would follow one of the trails instead of striking out across country, so he rode a short distance along each of them, searching for her horse's tracks.

He found them on the third trail he tried, the one that headed most directly south. Looked like maybe she was making for the high lonesome after all.

Of course she might still double back. Longarm kept his eyes open as he, too, rode south. Enough people used this trail so that it was clogged by a welter of tracks. He spotted Nicole's sign often enough, though, that he knew she was still going in this direction.

Around mid-morning he came to a shaft house perched on the side of a hill. The donkey engine that drew the ore cars out of the mine shaft rumbled and the stamp mill stamped. Longarm turned his horse and rode up to the mill. A door opened from a high porch into an office.

The door swung back as Longarm reined to a halt. A rawboned man in lace-up boots and heavy work clothes stepped out. He had a rifle tucked under his arm and a scowl tucked on his face.

"Not a very friendly welcome, old son."

"We've had a robbery here. We're not feeling very friendly."

Longarm's eyebrows rose. "Lose some ore?"

"No. Some supplies and clothes, a rifle, and some

money. We don't keep much cash on hand, but the bastard got all of it."

"You the mine superintendent?"

"That's right. Henry Cartland's the name. Who are you, mister, and what are you doing here?"

Longarm identified himself. "I'm looking for a fugitive who murdered a man in Virginia City. You might've heard of him—Harvey Kellogg."

"Kellogg's dead? Good Lord! Of course I've heard of him. He owns one of the largest banks in Virginia City. The syndicate that owns this mine does business with him. Did business with him, I guess I should say." Cartland dropped the scowl. "Come on into the office, Marshal. Got coffee on the stove. I'll bet the son of a bitch who broke in here last night was the same man who murdered Kellogg."

"Same person, maybe." Longarm swung down from the saddle, looped the reins around the railing that bordered the steep steps. "Not the same *man*, though . . .'cause it was a woman who ventilated Kellogg."

Cartland stared at him. "A *woman*?"

"That's right." Longarm climbed the steps. "Name of Nicole Gardner. Heard of her?"

Cartland scratched his lantern jaw. "Seems like I recollect hearing something about Kellogg courting some younger woman. He was a widower, or so I've heard. I didn't really know the man. Recognized him when I saw him on the street, but that's about all."

Longarm and Cartland went into the mine office. The whole building vibrated in time to the workings of the massive apparatus in the adjacent stamp mill. Cartland filled two cups with coffee from the pot simmering on the stove and handed one of them to Longarm.

"Why in the world would a gal who was about to marry a rich man like Kellogg up and murder him? That doesn't make any sense, Marshal."

"This particular woman's got a history of getting close to wealthy older men and sometimes even getting engaged to them before taking off with their money."

"Oh." Cartland nodded. "Like that, was it?"

"Yeah. I was on her trail to start with. I got to Virginia City, found out she was involved with Kellogg, and went to Kellogg's house to arrest her. Got there just as all hell broke loose. She'd shot Kellogg twice in the head and came damned close to killing his secretary, too."

"Lord have mercy. It doesn't seem right that a woman could do something like that. I guess in your line of work, though, Marshal, you see all kinds of folks who'll do just about anything."

Longarm inclined his head. "I've seen more'n my share of killers, that's for sure, Mr. Cartland. It's probably a good thing she didn't run into anybody here last night while she was stealing those things. Reckon she would've shot down anybody who got in her way."

"Of course, you don't *know* it was her who broke in here."

"The tracks of the horse she stole led here."

Cartland's eyes widened. "A horse thief, too? Damn, that young lady really is a criminal." He thought about it for a second. "You say she's been going around swindling older gentlemen?"

"That's right."

"No offense, Marshal, but it seems like that's sort of an odd crime for a federal lawman to be taking an interest in."

Longarm wasn't going to go into any detail about Nicole Gardner's last victim before coming to Virginia City. The congressman would want his involvement with her kept quiet, especially since she'd wound up fleecing him. An embarrassment like that could prove damaging to a political career.

"All I know is my boss gave me the job." Longarm drank some more of the coffee, which was black and stout enough

42

to get up and walk around on its own hind legs. Mighty good, in other words. "Tell me again what all got stolen."

Cartland went through the list, which included a pair of corduroy trousers, a couple of flannel shirts, a jacket and slouch hat, a pair of work boots and socks.

"Sounds like a whole outfit."

Cartland nodded. "All the clothes belonged to me. Spares, mostly, but I hate to lose them anyway. And that was my best jacket she got off with, blast it."

"What about the rifle?"

"A new Winchester." Cartland gestured toward a rack on the wall where several rifles hung. "We keep several of them around here, mostly in case any wolves venture too close. She took a box of ammunition from the desk, too, when she took the money from the cash box."

"You said something about supplies?"

Cartland nodded again. "She got into the cook shack and filled up a sack with flour and sugar and salt and bacon. Enough to keep her from starving for several days. Maybe as long as a week."

Longarm didn't like any of what he was hearing. He hadn't gotten too good a look at what Nicole was wearing when she fled from the Kellogg mansion. He thought it was some sort of flimsy nightdress. Catching up to a scared, half-dressed woman riding bareback on a stolen horse with no gear had sounded pretty easy. The job got harder now that she was dressed, provisioned, and armed. And even though Cartland was right about not being absolutely certain Nicole was behind the theft at the mine, Longarm's gut told him it was true. Not only that, but steady nerves had been required for such a robbery.

Capturing Nicole Gardner was shaping up to be a bigger challenge than Longarm had first expected.

"You're not missing any horses?"

"No, we've only got a few saddle mounts here and nobody bothered them."

"What about those saddles?"

Cartland shook his head. "They're all here."

So Nicole was still riding the horse she had taken from the stable behind Kellogg's mansion, and riding bareback, to boot. Maybe she didn't mind doing that.

Maybe there was more to her than just a money-hungry adventuress.

"What are you going to do, Marshal?"

Longarm drained the last of his coffee and handed the cup back to the mine superintendent. "Reckon I'll go after her. That's my job, after all."

"If you recover any of the things she stole from us . . ."

"Yeah?"

Cartland gave a humorless laugh. "Don't bring 'em back. I'd just as soon the story not get around that we were robbed by a female desperado."

Chapter 8

Longarm asked Cartland a few more questions about the area to the south. The hills gave way to a stretch of flat, semiarid terrain that was next thing to a desert. A mountain range jutted up from that flatland after about twenty miles. The hills were dotted with mines but the flats were barren. The closest settlement was in the mountains to the south, a place called Antelope.

"It's not very big, though. Started out as a boomtown but the boom didn't last. The Comstock doesn't quite get down that far. But there are a few smaller mines in the area. If the woman didn't swing west toward Carson City, she must be heading for Antelope."

"I'm obliged for the information. Reckon I'd better be riding."

"Be careful, Marshal. I didn't much like the way the sky looked this morning. Could be we're in for a snowstorm."

Longarm had thought the same thing himself when he gazed at the gunmetal-gray heavens. When he stepped out of the mine office, they didn't look any better.

But he had a hunch that Nicole Gardner wasn't going to let the weather slow her down. So neither could he.

Longarm had the feeling during the day that the storm was following him. The wind from the north blew harder and colder. He was glad he was riding south. It would have stung like blazes to ride into the teeth of such a wind. As it was, he was chilled to the bone.

He found enough tracks left by Nicole's horse to know that he was still on the right trail. If the wind blew like this all night, though, it would wipe out most of the prints. Longarm felt a growing sense of urgency. He didn't want Nicole to slip away from him.

He came to the edge of the hills late that afternoon. On that last slope, about fifty yards from the trail, stood an old shack. Smoke curled from the stovepipe that jutted up from the roof. That told Longarm someone lived there. He angled toward the shack. Maybe its occupant could tell him whether or not Nicole had passed by recently.

Longarm was about halfway between the trail and the shack when the door of the run-down building swung back a few inches. He opened his mouth to give a hail and let the person inside the shack know that he was friendly.

Before any sound could come from him, a rifle barrel stuck out the door. Flame spat from the muzzle as the weapon went off with a wicked crack.

Longarm heard the wind rip of a bullet past his ear as he kicked his feet from the stirrups and flung himself out of the saddle. He hit the ground hard enough to jolt the breath from his body. The horse gave a neigh of fear and bolted, leaving him there.

Longarm rolled to the side and hunted cover behind a low rock. The rifle barked again. This time the bullet ricocheted off the rock where Longarm had taken shelter.

"Damn it, hold your fire! I'm a friend! Hold your fire!"

He knew better than to identify himself as a lawman right off. Some folks would just try harder to kill him if they knew he was a star packer.

The horse ran most of the way back to the trail before stopping. The Winchester was still in the saddle boot. Might as well be in China for all the good it was going to do Longarm now. He'd be cut down in less than ten paces if he made an attempt for the rifle.

Anyway, he didn't want to fight whoever was in the shack. He just wanted them to stop shooting at him.

Another bullet whined off the rock. Longarm took his hat off, put it on the barrel of his Colt, edged it upward so that the rifleman in the shack could see it. Sure enough, the hat went flying through the air as a bullet clipped a small chunk out of the brim.

Longarm didn't move. The hat lay in plain sight of the shack now.

Curiosity did what assurances of friendship had not. The shooting stopped. Longarm didn't make a sound as the cold wind swept over him.

A faint creak of hinges told him the door of the shack had opened farther. With the wind behind him he was lucky to hear that. He waited with the patience of Job and finally was rewarded by the faint scuff of boot leather on the rocky ground. A little closer, old son. Just come a little closer . . .

"What in blue blazes—"

The rifleman had come close enough to see him now. Longarm leaped to his feet and flung himself forward before the exclamation was finished. He tackled the portly shape wrapped in a thick coat, drove it backward off its feet. The old Henry rifle the shack dweller carried went flying in the air.

Longarm crashed to the ground with the rifleman underneath him. He drove a knee into the man's stomach. His right fist rose, ready to smash down into the man's face.

The blow didn't fall. An old man with a round, cherubic

face that reminded Longarm of Billy Vail's stared up at him, eyes wide with fear.

"Don't hurt me, mister!" The words came out in a high-pitched croak. "Please don't hurt me!"

"A fine thing to say when you damn near blew my head off!"

"I . . . I wasn't really tryin' to hit you! I meant no harm, honest!"

Longarm knew better. This old pelican had done his damnedest to ventilate him. Longarm had luck and good reflexes to thank for the fact that he was still alive.

But he wasn't in the habit of beating up on fellas old enough to be his grandpa, no matter what they'd done. He pushed himself to his feet and drew the Colt again to cover the old-timer as he stepped back.

"Get up. Don't try anything funny."

"No, sir, I won't. I sure won't."

The old man stood up awkwardly. His hat had come off when Longarm tackled him. A few wisps of white hair tangled around his bald head. He was a full head shorter than Longarm.

"Who are you?"

The old-timer kept his hands up as Longarm covered him. "Name's Quinn, Pete Quinn."

Longarm looked at the man's rough, tattered work clothes and made a guess. "Prospector, are you?"

"Yes, sir. I been huntin' for silver in these hills for nigh on to twenty years now."

"Find any?"

"Not so's you'd notice."

"Good Lord. We're on the edge of the Comstock Lode. How could you *not* find silver?"

Pete Quinn shrugged. "Bad luck? Some fellas just ain't cut out to get rich, I guess, no matter how hard they try."

"How do you get by?"

"I work up at the mines some. Odd jobs. Guide folks

across the desert sometimes. I know where all the water holes are."

"Why'd you shoot at me? Just naturally proddy, are you?"

Quinn looked offended for the first time. "No, sir, I ain't. I thought you'd come to rob me, just like that other fella."

Longarm's interest quickened. "What other fella? When did this happen?"

"Earlier today. Son of a bitch took my saddle. I got a old mule I ride sometimes. Saddle weren't much but it was the onliest one I had."

Longarm gestured with the barrel of the Colt. "Put your hands down. You ain't gonna try to shoot me again, are you?"

"No, sir, not if you ain't a thief like that other fella."

"Well, I'm not." Longarm picked up the Henry rifle. "I'll just hang onto this for the time being, however. For safekeeping, I reckon you could say. Come on while I catch my horse. I want to talk to you some more."

"I'm glad to talk. Don't get many visitors out here."

"I can see why, what with those hot-lead welcomes."

A sheepish grin wreathed Quinn's round face. "Aw, that was a mistake. I just flew off the handle 'cause I was still ticked about gettin' robbed earlier. I don't shoot at ever'body who rides by, I swear."

Longarm hoped not.

He caught the horse he'd rented back in Virginia City and led the animal over to the shack. Pete Quinn came with him. The old-timer gestured at the rickety building.

"Come on inside. We'll get out o' this cold wind. Sorry I don't have no whiskey or anything else to offer you."

"That's all right." Once they were inside it was warmer, although the chilly wind whistled through cracks in the walls. An old stove gave off a little heat.

Longarm asked Quinn to describe the robber. Even

though Quinn had referred to the thief as a man, Longarm thought it was pretty likely to have been Nicole Gardner, continuing her crime spree.

"Well, he was sort of a short fella. Had his britches' legs rolled up a couple o' turns."

That matched up with Cartland's story. The mining man had said that the stolen trousers were his, and he was considerably taller than Nicole.

"Had on a jacket with the collar turned up and a slouch hat pulled down low so I didn't really get a good look at his face. He waved a rifle at me and told me to put my saddle on that horse he'd been ridin' bareback."

That cinched it in Longarm's mind. "What sort of voice did he have?"

"Come to think of it, it was a mite high-pitched." Quinn laughed. "Like mine but even more, maybe."

"That's because the fella who stole your saddle was really a woman."

Quinn goggled at him. "A woman! Well, I'll swan. You sure about that?"

Longarm nodded. "Yeah, I'm sure."

"Well, I wish I'd knowed that. First woman who's been here on this place in a hell of a long time, I'll tell you that." Quinn shook his head in amazement.

"Which way was she going when she rode off?"

"She headed south across the desert toward the mountains." A shrewd look came into Quinn's rheumy old eyes. "You're chasin' her, ain't you?"

"Yeah."

"She your sweetheart . . . or are you a lawman?"

Longarm didn't see any harm in admitting it now. "Deputy U.S. marshal. And I never actually met the gal, so we ain't sweethearts."

"Well, I'll tell you one thing, Marshal . . . You better be careful."

"Why's that?"

"I seen the look in her eyes when she pointed that rifle at me." Quinn shook his head. "Woman or not, if you cross that one, Marshal . . . she'll shoot you soon as look at you."

Chapter 9

It was too late in the day for Longarm to start across the flats toward the mountains. If he did, night would overtake him out there in the middle of nowhere without any shelter. So whether he liked it or not, the sensible thing to do was to stay here in Pete Quinn's ramshackle cabin until morning.

The old prospector didn't care. In fact he was eager to curry favor with a lawman, so he asked Longarm to spend the night.

"I got enough vittles for us both, if you ain't hungrier for anything fancier'n beans and cornbread."

"Beans and cornbread will be fine, old-timer. I'll throw in some bacon from my saddlebags."

Quinn licked his lips. "I like bacon. I'm obliged to you, Marshal."

Quinn built up the fire and made it a little more comfortable in the shack's single room. The wind whipping through the cracks in the walls kept it from getting too warm.

Living out here in the middle of nowhere as he did, Quinn was hungry for conversation. He wanted to know all about the woman Longarm was pursuing. The old-timer listened in rapt attention as Longarm explained what he knew about Nicole Gardner and her criminal career under various names.

"You say she's pretty?" Quinn's voice held a wistful tone.

"I just caught a glimpse of her, but she looked pretty nice to me. And she wouldn't have been able to trick all those men into giving her money if she was ugly."

"No, I reckon not." Quinn sighed. "If I was a rich man, it might be worth it to have a pretty gal makin' a fuss over me. Been a hell of a long time since a gal even smiled at me, let alone stroked my forehead and told me I was her sweet baby."

"You wouldn't like it if she did that and then ran off with a bunch of your money, though."

"I don't know." Quinn shook his head. "I just don't know. Man does without havin' a gal around for long enough, he's liable to put up with just about anything. That's what I meant when I said it might be worth it."

Longarm didn't think so, but the old-timer could believe whatever he wanted to believe.

While Quinn prepared their rough supper, Longarm went outside and led the rented horse around to the back of the shack. An open shed leaned against the building and blocked the north wind. Quinn's swaybacked old nag was out there so Longarm put his horse in the shed, too. He unsaddled it and poured some grain into a shallow trough. The cold was really settling in. Longarm's breath fogged in front of his face.

He went back inside, ate supper with Quinn. Then Longarm spread his bedroll on the floor and crawled into his blankets. He wasn't going to put the prospector out of the long sagging bunk. Quinn blew out the single lantern that lit the room. All that was left was the cherry-red glow around the door in the potbellied stove.

That glow faded as the fire died down. Longarm got up after a while, opened the stove door, and fed more wood

into it until the flames were crackling again. Quinn continued to snore as he had started doing a couple of minutes
after he turned in for the night.

As Longarm lay there trying to ignore the chill and go
to sleep, he thought about the case so far. Luck had been
with him at first. He had found the woman he was looking
for without any trouble.

But then her scheme to swindle Harvey Kellogg had
blown up in her face just as Longarm arrived at the mansion. A coincidence like that and bad luck went hand in
hand. The woman currently calling herself Nicole Gardner
had fled and so far she had managed to give him the slip.
Now she had not only a horse but also clothes, supplies, a
saddle . . . and a gun.

So far she'd shown no qualms about resorting to robbery to get what she needed. Longarm had no doubt that
if she found herself in need of something else, she would
steal and maybe even kill again to acquire it. If she reached
the settlement in the mountains, she could restock on
supplies there. Then it would be off into the mountains,
and Longarm might have a devil of a time tracking her
down.

She was no weak, pampered city gal—he was sure of
that now. At some time in her past she had lived a hard-
scrabble existence, had learned how to survive no matter
what it took. He had thought starting out that catching her
would be an easy chore, but he was beginning to understand that might not be the case.

Sleep stole over him while he was contemplating all
that. Some time later he roused from that slumber, listen-
ing closely in order to figure out what had awakened him.
All he heard was the howling of the wind and Pete Quinn
snoring as loud as ever . . .

Louder, in fact. And closer. Too close.

Longarm's eyes snapped open. The glow from the stove

was down to almost nothing. It was just enough to show a dark figure looming over him. The old prospector was awake but still snoring. Doing it deliberately so Longarm wouldn't wake up.

The rustle of clothing warned Longarm to move.

He rolled to the side. The snoring stopped as Quinn grunted with effort. Something hit the floor with a loud *thunk*! The red glow of the dying fire reflected off the head of an ax. It had landed where Longarm's head was a second earlier.

Quinn had struck with such force that the ax was embedded in the floorboard. He cursed as he wrenched the weapon in an effort to free it.

Longarm kicked upward and buried the heel of his boot in Quinn's ample belly. The prospector groaned and doubled over. Hurt but enraged, he finally got the ax free and slashed at Longarm with it.

Longarm rolled again to avoid the blow. When he came up again, he had the Colt in his hand.

"Damn it, drop that ax, Quinn! I'll shoot!"

Quinn lunged at him. The ax whistled through the air again. Longarm pulled the trigger.

Flame geysered from the Colt's muzzle. The bullet struck Quinn and flung him backward. The ax flew from his hands. But it was already coming forward and kept going. Longarm felt the razor-sharp edge of the blade bite into his left arm.

He gritted his teeth against the pain, came to his feet. Quinn lay on the floor, breathing heavily. The breathing had a wet blubbery sound to it. Longarm stepped over to him. Kept the pistol trained on Quinn as he knelt next to the prospector.

"What the hell was that all about? Why'd you try to cleave my head open, Quinn?"

The old-timer was hit bad. The sound of his breathing meant that at least one lung was ventilated. He wouldn't make it, but for now he clung to life with stubborn determination.

"Figured I could . . . keep what I wanted from your outfit . . . and sell the rest . . . along with the horse."

"You couldn't have sold the horse in Virginia City. It came from the livery stable there. Somebody would've recognized it."

"Didn't plan to . . . go to Virginia City. Folks in Antelope . . . don't care . . . where somethin' came from."

Longarm's face hardened. "You're saying the town's run by outlaws?"

Quinn didn't answer. "You got so much . . . and I got so little . . . Never had no luck . . . worked hard all those years . . . with not a blessed thing to show for it. Ain't fair. Just . . . ain't fair."

"So you thought you had a right to murder me and steal my gear?"

"That gal . . . stole from me . . . me, who's got nothin'. And you got so much. . . ." A long sigh came from Quinn. He didn't say anything else.

Longarm slipped a hand inside Quinn's coat, felt for a pulse. Didn't find one. But he found the wet stickiness where his bullet had bored into Quinn's chest.

A gust of wind rattled the shack's walls. Longarm got to his feet, put more wood in the stove. He left the stove door open for a minute to let more heat and light into the room.

That didn't change anything. Quinn was still dead for no good reason. He had been robbed so he had tried to rob somebody else in turn. And all it had gotten him was a bullet.

Of course it was possible that the old-timer had been robbing and even murdering folks who passed through here for a long time. Or maybe this was the first instance of him straying from the straight and narrow in his whole life. Longarm didn't know, and likely never would. But Quinn hadn't given him a choice. If Longarm had waited to act, he would probably be the one who was dead now.

Knowing that didn't help much. Sharing the shack with the old prospector's corpse meant that it was going to be a long time until morning.

Chapter 10

The overcast sky was still there when Longarm opened the door of the shack the next morning. Thick gray clouds scudded through the sky, driven by the cold wind. Snow had fallen during the night. The powdery white stuff dusted the ground and had blown into drifts several inches deep in places. A few flurries still came down.

Longarm found a shovel in the shed with the horses and started digging a grave for Pete Quinn. Even though the delay chafed at him, he couldn't just ride off without giving the old prospector a proper burial. Not even the fact that Quinn had tried to kill him would prompt Longarm to do that.

The ground was hard and rocky but not yet frozen. Longarm labored with the shovel until he was hot and sweaty under the sheepskin jacket. His left arm was stiff and sore from the cut the ax had left in it. He had cleaned the wound with whiskey the night before, wrapped it up real good with strips of cloth. He thought it would heal all right, but it was going to be a hindrance for a while.

When the shallow grave was deep enough, he brought the blanket-wrapped body out of the shack. Lowered it into the grave. Shoveled the dirt back in.

When he was finished, he leaned on the shovel and took his hat off for a moment, sent up a prayer that El Señor Dios would take the old-timer into His heavenly hacienda if He saw fit. That was all Longarm could do for Pete Quinn.

He turned the prospector's old nag out of the shed. There were quite a few mines, small and large, in these hills. It was likely the horse would drift over to one of them. If anybody recognized it and came looking for Quinn, they would find the fresh grave.

Longarm saddled his own mount. He took the coffee from Quinn's shack but left everything else. He wasn't a thief but he wasn't going to let a perfectly good bag of Arbuckle's go to waste, either.

Then he started across the flats toward the gray bulk of the mountains in the distance.

A feeling of bleakness had begun to grow inside him. Nicole Gardner hadn't been so far ahead of him that she could have gotten all the way across this near-desert the day before. Night would have caught her out here in the open. She'd had no shelter from the wind and snow. Longarm wasn't going to be a bit surprised if he found her frozen body somewhere up ahead.

Even though the layer of snow on the ground was thin, it covered any tracks that were left. Longarm steered a course as due south as he could manage, figuring that his quarry would have continued in that direction. If Nicole had veered off, she was going to get that much more of a lead on him. Nothing he could do about it now.

And that was assuming she'd lived through the night. Longarm thought the odds of that were slim.

Around mid-morning he spotted a dark shape against the white of the snow. A man could see a long way out here on the flats. Whatever the dark thing might be, it was a good quarter of a mile away. And since it didn't seem to be going anywhere, Longarm didn't get in a hurry.

The thing wasn't Nicole Gardner. It was a horse.

A dead horse with its belly cut wide open.

Longarm reined in and frowned down at the remains. One of the horse's forelegs was bent at an odd angle. Nicole must have been running the animal hard when it stepped in a hole or something and broke its leg. Maybe she'd been trying to reach the mountains before darkness closed in on her. If so the effort had backfired.

She'd been stuck out here with a horse that couldn't be ridden. With night and a snowstrom bearing down on her.

Once again she had done the only thing she could to survive.

Longarm dismounted, looked closer at the horse, found the black-rimmed bullethole in its head. Nicole had put the animal out of its misery. Cartland, the mine superintendent, hadn't said anything about Nicole stealing a knife, but obviously she had. She'd slit the horse's belly open, raked out enough of the guts to make a space for herself, and crawled inside to spend the night. There would have been a little warmth left in the body and it sheltered her from the wind at the same time. That had been enough to allow her to make it through until morning.

The snow had covered up most of the offal she had pulled from the body. But it revealed her footprints leading off to the south. Longarm wasn't going to have much trouble following the trail now. And since she was afoot and he was mounted . . .

Well, the chase had gotten a mite easier again.

The dead horse still had Pete Quinn's old saddle on it but that was all. The supplies Nicole had stolen from the mine were gone. That meant she was carrying them. That burden would slow her down even more. Longarm swung up into the saddle, heeled his mount into a walk. No need to hurry all that much now.

Nicole's tracks wavered some but generally ran pretty straight. The wind swirled around Longarm and pelted him with snow flurries from time to time as he followed the footprints. Hard to tell what time it was since the sun was invisible behind the clouds and he didn't want to open his coat to dig his watch out. The snow changed from flurries to a hard steady fall. That cut down on how far he could see.

Didn't matter. As long as he could see the tracks, he could follow Nicole's trail. He thought there was still a chance he might find her dead before he reached the mountains. She might have collapsed from exhaustion and succumbed to the elements.

The blizzard that had been looming for several days finally broke during the afternoon. Longarm hunched forward in the saddle as icy wind buffeted him and a thick white curtain of blowing snow filled the air. Within minutes after the full force of the storm hit, the snow seemed to be falling sideways. Longarm was just about blind. He couldn't see Nicole's tracks anymore, couldn't even see where he was going. But he couldn't stop, either, because that would doom him. He hoped he was still heading toward the mountains. If he reached them, he might be able to find a place where he could get out of the storm.

It galled him to give up his pursuit of the fugitive. But he could pick up Nicole's trail later. He would never bring her to justice if he was dead.

Longarm plodded along for what seemed like hours before he realized that his horse was moving uphill. He looked around, barely made out the dark shapes of pine trees. He had made it across the flats and reached the foothills. Now all he had to do was find a place to hole up and wait out the storm. Then he could start looking for Nicole Gardner again.

He had probably passed her during the blizzard, he thought. Her snow-covered body would lie out there until the sun came out and melted the snow to reveal the frozen corpse.

It wasn't the outcome Longarm would have wanted but it was justice of a sort, he supposed.

He found a low sandstone bluff with its base screened by several trees. The trees would help cut the wind and the bluff was sort of concave, so he thought he might be able to build a fire underneath it. Even a small blaze would help thaw him out.

He turned the horse toward the bluff, rode through the trees, reined in. He swung his right leg over the animal's back to the ground, but his left foot was still in the stirrup when a voice called out over the noise of the wind.

"Don't move!"

Longarm stayed where he was. He didn't have much choice with his foot in the stirrup like that. If he tried to move too fast, it would get caught. If the horse bolted, he would wind up being dragged.

And surprise rooted him there as well, because the voice that had issued the order belonged to a woman.

Longarm turned his head. In the snowstorm and the fading light he could see only about fifteen feet. That was enough for him to be able to make out the figure pointing a rifle at him. In the work clothes and thick jacket and slouch hat the figure wasn't womanly at all, but Longarm's gut told him it was Nicole Gardner who had the drop on him.

Lord, she was one tough gal!

"Where the hell did you come from?" Longarm couldn't contain the exclamation.

"You rode right past me!"

Yep, that was what he'd thought might happen.

"So I followed you! I hoped you knew where you were going! But even if you didn't, it was easier to follow you after your horse had broken a trail through the snow!"

"How about letting me finish getting down from this horse?"

"Who are you? Why are you following me?"

Telling the truth right now would be a good way of getting himself shot. She didn't have to know that he was a lawman—or that she was his quarry.

63

"Following you? What the hell are you talking about, lady? I'm just trying to find a place to get out of this damn blizzard!"

"What's your name?"

"Parker!"

"Well, Mr. Parker, I'm a woman alone and I won't hesitate to shoot you if you try anything funny. Go ahead and dismount. You think you can build a fire under that bluff?"

"I sure intend to try. I'm about half-froze!"

He took his foot out of the stirrup, stepped away from the horse. Nicole still had the drop on him now, but as long as she didn't know who he was he could afford to bide his time. When the right moment came, he could take that rifle away from her.

Problem with that plan was that he might not get the chance to wait. Several more shapes appeared at the top of the bluff just as the wind died down enough for him to hear the metallic sound of guns being cocked. A harsh voice shouted an order.

"Kill 'em! Kill 'em both!"

Chapter 11

Longarm had no idea who the newcomers were but it didn't really matter. The sons of bitches opened fire on him and Nicole. Flame spouted from the muzzles of their weapons and lead fanged through the snow-filled air. Hot bullets sizzled into the drifts.

Nicole's rifle blasted as Longarm threw himself to the side and into some drifted snow. His hand went under his coat and came out with the .45 from the cross-draw rig. He rolled over in the drift and came up on a knee. The Colt bucked in his hand as he triggered it.

The wind and the snow muffled the shots so that they sounded a bit like the thunder of distant drums. Up above, one of the men doubled over and plunged off the bluff. He landed with a hard thud not far from Longarm and didn't move again.

Longarm didn't know where Nicole was, didn't know if she had been wounded in that opening volley. Her rifle kept firing so he assumed she was all right. Another of the killers on the bluff twisted around and slumped to the ground. Maybe Longarm had hit him, maybe Nicole had. Didn't matter as long as the bastard was out of the fight.

White-hot pain slammed into Longarm's side. He went over backward. He knew he had been hit hard.

But he didn't lose consciousness and he didn't drop his gun. The Colt still had a couple of rounds in it. Gritting his teeth against the pain, he lined up the barrel on one of the snow-shrouded figures and pulled the trigger again. The man flipped backward. Longarm caught a glimpse of a splash of red: blood from a bullet-torn throat.

Then blackness flowed like ink through the white of the snowstorm. Longarm couldn't feel the cold anymore. That was bad. It meant he couldn't feel much of anything.

Except the heat in his side where the bullet had struck him. *That* he could feel.

And it was the last thing he was aware of as the darkness flowed over him.

He awoke to more heat but this time it was accompanied by the crackling of flames. It beat against him, brought him back from oblivion.

He forced his eyes open. He was lying on his left side and the fire was about five feet away. Small but burning fiercely. Beyond it, snow still swirled through the air. An occasional flake reached the fire and died with a hiss.

Longarm's right side hurt like hell. A burning, throbbing pain that threatened to overwhelm his senses. He pushed it away, forced his brain to ignore it and work on comprehending his surroundings instead. Something cold pressed against his back. He lifted his head, tried to look behind him. A rock wall loomed there.

He was inside the little cavelike overhang at the base of the bluff. He figured that out after a moment.

But who had dragged him over here? And how bad was he wounded? Had he been brought into this makeshift shelter just to die?

In addition to the heat, the fire cast a circle of yellow light tinged with red. A figure stomped through the snow and came into that circle of light. Nicole. Longarm recognized the stolen clothes even though she had a woolen scarf wrapped around the lower half of her face. With the slouch hat pulled down, all that was visible were her eyes.

The horse crowded against the sandstone bluff, eager to get out of the snow and wind. There was no place to tie the animal, but it didn't look like it was going anywhere as long as the storm raged. Nicole hunkered on her heels across the fire from Longarm. He watched her through slitted eyes.

Not slitted enough. "I know you're awake, mister. I felt you watching me when I brought the horse in."

So she was pretty observant. That didn't surprise Longarm. Her life as a swindler and thief must have honed her senses to a razor-sharp keenness.

He opened his eyes all the way. "Those bastards who jumped us?"

"Dead." Her voice was flat and just about as cold as the wind. "Except maybe for one. I'm not sure. I don't know how many of them there were."

Neither did Longarm. He had seen at least four men up there on top of the bluff.

"How many corpses you got?" He figured she had checked them to make sure they were all dead.

"Four."

"That's all I counted. Might've been a fifth man, though."

"I think there was. I found some blood on the snow where none of the bodies were."

"So he was hit. Weather like this, he probably won't get very far. He'll curl up and die."

"We can hope."

Longarm chuckled despite the pain and disorientation he felt. "Mighty tough, ain't you?"

"Tough enough, Mr. Parker."

"How bad am I hit?"

She stood up and came closer to him. "I'd better find

out. I haven't had a chance to look at your wound yet. I pulled you in here, built the fire, then went to see about your horse and those dead men."

"You done right. We need that horse. And we didn't need any of those gunmen turning out not to be dead. That's a good way to get taken by surprise and killed."

She knelt beside him. "The way you're talking it sounds like your mind's clear. Maybe you're not hurt too bad."

Longarm tensed as Nicole reached out to pull his sheepskin coat back. If she searched him, she might find the leather folder containing his badge and identification papers. That would ruin his idea of pretending to be just a drifter named Parker.

She didn't seem interested in going through his pockets. She opened his coat and pulled his shirt up to expose the wound. Some of the blood had already dried—or already frozen, maybe. Either way, it stuck when she lifted the shirt and he grimaced and sucked his breath in through his teeth as she pulled it loose.

"Sorry."

"No, don't mind me. Just see what needs to be done."

A moment passed while she studied his wounded side by the light of the fire.

"It doesn't look too bad. The wound is more than a graze but it's pretty shallow. The bullet went in and right back out. Took a little chunk of meat with it." Another pause. "Judging by the scars on your body, this isn't the first time you've been shot."

"Nope. I'm sorry to say it ain't."

"Then you know I've got to clean out the wound or else risk it festering."

Longarm lifted a hand toward the horse. "Bottle of Tom Moore in the saddlebags." He had brought the Maryland rye with him from Virginia City. Hadn't pulled the cork on it yet. Now it was going to come in handy for medicinal purposes. Nicole might give him a little nip of it, too.

She stood and went to the horse, reached into the saddlebags, and found the bottle. As she came back to the fire, she pulled the cork with her teeth and spat it into her other hand. Tilted the bottle to her mouth and took a swig.

Longarm had to grin. Nicole might be a swindler and a murderer but she had her good qualities, too.

She knelt beside him. "This is going to hurt like blazes. You want a slug first?"

"I'd be much obliged."

She put her free hand under his head, raised it so he could drink when she held the bottle to his lips. "Don't guzzle too much. You want to leave enough so I can clean out that bullet hole."

Longarm took a short drink, sighed in satisfaction as he felt the warm glow of the rye whiskey in his gullet and then in his stomach.

"Go ahead."

She poured the liquor right through the hole in his side—she wasn't stingy with it either. It might as well have been a blazing torch, the way it felt.

Longarm let out a groan and sucked in his breath again. The pain slowly began to recede.

"I'm going to bandage it up now as best I can. That's all I can do for you. You'll need some medical attention from a real doctor to make sure the wound heals up all right."

Drowsiness stole over Longarm as she tore strips from his shirt, wadded a couple of them into pads, used the others to tie the pads in place over the entrance and exit wounds. "Might be a sawbones . . . in Antelope."

"Where's that?"

"Settlement up in the hills . . . south o' here."

"That's the way I was going. I didn't know there was a town there. Thank you for telling me about it."

A normal man would be mighty curious about her by now. Longarm didn't want her to get suspicious of him. "Who are you? What're you doing out here . . . in this blizzard?"

"You can call me Nicole. It's as good a name as any." She stood up. "But what I'm doing out here is none of your business, Mr. Parker. All that matters is that I've done what I can for you and now I have to leave."

She turned away from the fire. Headed for Longarm's horse.

He pushed himself up on an elbow. "Wait just . . . just a damned minute. You can't mean that you're gonna—"

"Steal your horse?" She didn't look around at him. "I'm afraid so. Good luck to you, Mr. Parker."

With that she took hold of the reins, put her foot in the stirrup, and swung up into the saddle. Longarm tried to push himself to his feet as Nicole turned the horse away from the bluff's sandstone wall. The wound in his side pulled painfully as he reached across his body for his gun.

The holster was empty. Damn.

"Good Lord! You can't just—"

Still she didn't look at him. "I don't have any choice. I left enough wood to keep the fire going all night."

With that she heeled the horse into a trot and disappeared into the snow-laden darkness. Longarm slumped back onto the ground. Weakness and exhaustion washed over him.

He hadn't seen *that* coming. But knowing what he did about Nicole, he should have. Of course she'd abandoned him and saved herself. That was her nature.

As he slipped once more into unconsciousness, his last thought was that this was going to make it harder to catch her again and arrest her.

Harder . . . but not impossible. Not as long as he was alive.

Chapter 12

When Longarm came to again, he thought the pain from his wound must be causing him to imagine things.

He smelled bacon cooking.

His eyes flickered open. He saw Nicole kneeling beside the fire, frying bacon in a little pan she had taken from his saddlebags. It smelled so good he wondered for a second if they had bacon in heaven. He figured he'd ask Saint Peter about that if he ever got as far as the Pearly Gates, which was sort of doubtful considering the life he'd led.

"You came back." His voice was a dry croak.

"I'm a damned fool, that's what I am. I started worrying that you might not wake up in time to keep the fire from going out. Then you'd freeze and you'd never wake up."

"I'm . . . obliged." He looked past her, saw the gray light of dawn spreading over the snow-covered landscape. The weather had let up for the moment but the stark gray sky held the promise of more precipitation. "It's morning?"

"Yes. Do you want some bacon?"

"More than just about anything else in the world right now."

She set the pan at the edge of the fire, came over to him. "Let me help you sit up."

She got her arms around him and lifted his body. He was a big man, so he knew it couldn't be easy for her. She managed, though, and soon he was propped up against the sandstone wall. The bacon had cooled quickly in the frigid air. She handed him a piece of it. His right arm worked all right despite the soreness in his side. He lifted the bacon to his mouth and took a bite.

Yeah. Worthy of heaven, all right.

Now that it was light, Nicole built up the fire even more. She didn't have to worry about it being seen. Longarm knew that was the natural caution of a fugitive coming out in her. He ate more of the bacon, reveled in the warmth of the flames. He almost felt human again.

"What are you running from?" Of course he knew the answer but he asked the question anyway. He wanted to see what she was going to say.

She frowned at him. "What makes you think I'm running from anything?"

"Well, you stole my horse last night and were ready to ride off and leave me here. That strikes me as the actions of a pretty desperate woman. I figured somebody must be chasing you to make you act like that."

"I *did* come back, you know."

"Yeah, and you said that made you a damned fool, too. Like it meant that something was gaining on you."

"You're too nosy, Mr. Parker."

Longarm managed to shrug. "There's a good chance you saved my life, ma'am. That's why I'm curious about you."

That was true. Even though he knew the facts, he wanted to know more about her. Maybe he wanted to know *why* she did the things she'd done.

If that was the case, he was disappointed. Her answer was vague. "People think I did something I didn't do. It was easier to run than to stay and try to explain things."

Longarm lifted a hand and moved it to take in their

72

surroundings. "Seems like almost anything would've been better than this."

"That just shows what you know. And nobody told me there was going to be a blasted blizzard."

Longarm nodded. He wasn't going to press the issue. Not now, when he was wounded and in bad shape and still a ways from the nearest settlement. Time enough to get Nicole Gardner's side of the story later . . . although he couldn't imagine what she might be able to tell him that would change his mind about what she had done. Murder was murder.

"What happened to those hombres who threw down on us? One of 'em fell off the bluff but I don't see his body anywhere around here."

"The wolves took care of it. One of them was dragging the body away when I came back. I heard others snapping and snarling among themselves up on top of the bluff where the other bodies were."

"Wolves, eh?"

"The fire was still burning. They wouldn't have bothered you."

"Unless the fire went out."

She shrugged. "Call it another reason I came back, along with outright stupidity."

"Well, ma'am, no offense, but I'm glad you were stupid enough to come along and save my life."

A few moments of silence went by before Nicole spoke again. "Those men must have had horses. When it gets a little lighter, I'll ride up there and see if I can find them. That way both of us can ride on to Antelope."

"That horse of mine might be able to carry double."

"I'm sure it could, but I don't want to wear it out before we get to the settlement."

"If there were wolves around, those horses probably spooked and stampeded clear back to wherever they came from."

"Maybe. But I'll see what I can find anyway."

Longarm didn't argue with her. He didn't think she would ride off and leave him again. Not after coming back like she had. If she truly didn't care whether he lived or died, she would have kept going.

But somebody could care about a stranger and still be capable of murder, he reminded himself.

Nicole ate the rest of the bacon, cleaned the pan with snow, and put it away in the saddlebags. She then mounted up and rode to the top of the bluff as she had said she was going to.

Longarm was surprised about half an hour later when she came back, leading another saddle horse behind her.

The scarf she wore drooped enough so he could see part of her grin. "Told you I might find one of them."

"Yeah, you did."

She dismounted, came over to him. "Let me help you up."

She took hold of his left arm. He winced.

Instantly she looked worried. "Are you wounded there, too? You didn't say anything about your left arm being hurt."

"It happened before, not during that shoot-out. Just a cut. Nothing to worry about."

"You're sure?"

"Yeah. Let's get out of here."

He pushed himself to his feet with her help. For a few seconds the world spun crazily around him before it settled down. When he felt steady enough, he moved stiffly toward the horse he had been riding.

"No, the other one is yours now." Nicole steered him toward the mount she had brought back. "That one doesn't have a Winchester strapped to the saddle."

"Speaking of guns, what happened to my Colt?"

"I have it." She paused and moved the tail of her jacket aside enough so that he could see the walnut butt of the

74

weapon, tucked behind the belt around her trim waist. "If you need it later, I'll give it back to you."

"If I need it, there might not be time for you to give it back."

She ignored his complaint and helped him climb up onto the second horse. The effort made a dull throb of pain go through him. He sat there in the saddle and took a couple of deep breaths. The pain eased somewhat.

"Are you all right to ride?"

"Sure. I been hurt worse'n this plenty of times."

"I know. I saw those scars, remember?"

Longarm didn't say anything to that. He didn't mind her seeing his scars as long as she hadn't seen his badge and bona fides. If she had . . . if she knew he was really a deputy United States marshal . . . it was doubtful that she would still be helping him.

He lifted the reins and heeled the horse into motion. They rode around the bluff and up a gentler slope. Even though the carcasses of the dead gunmen had been dragged off by wolves, Longarm could still see bright splashes of crimson on the snow, mute evidence of the deaths that had occurred earlier.

They rode south. Nicole seemed to have a good sense of direction. Longarm would have corrected their course if he'd needed to, but that necessity didn't arise.

A couple of hours after sunup found them through the foothills and into the mountains. There was no trail and the rugged landscape assured that they couldn't travel in a straight line anyway. They came across a narrow, fast-flowing creek and followed it. Longarm figured they never went more than a couple of hundred yards in any direction before making a sharp turn again.

Snow blanketed the piney slopes and the narrow valleys between the mountains. Longarm and Nicole climbed steadily. There had to be a pass up there somewhere ahead of them.

Longarm finally spotted a thin spiral of smoke in the air and pointed it out to Nicole. "That's probably coming from Antelope."

"Somebody lives over there anyway. We'll head in that direction."

Again Longarm didn't argue with her. Antelope probably had a town marshal or some other sort of lawman. With luck there'd be a jail there where he could lock up Nicole while he recuperated from his injuries for a spell. It was going to be a mite hard to put her behind bars after she'd saved his life that way.

Longarm figured he'd manage. It was his job, after all.

Chapter 13

Distances are deceptive in the mountains. It was nearly midday by the time Longarm and Nicole topped a ridge and looked down into the snow-covered valley where the settlement of Antelope lay. A pair of streets ran parallel, east and west, for a dozen blocks. Buildings ranged from tar-paper shacks on the edge of town to sturdy brick edifices in the center. Smoke came from quite a few chimneys but the wind dispersed it. The smoke Longarm had spotted earlier rose from a bonfire at the western end of town. Several men stood near the blaze, throwing something into it, but at this distance Longarm couldn't make out what it was they were burning.

He and Nicole started down the slope toward the settlement. Snow flurries had resumed a short while earlier. Longarm figured the blizzard would be back in full force by nightfall. He planned to be indoors tonight, and glad of it.

Nicole spoke when they were halfway down the hill. "Some of those buildings are boarded up."

"Antelope used to be a boomtown. There were silver mines all around in these mountains. The mines played out, though, sooner than the ones around Virginia City have."

"You've been here before?"

Longarm shook his head. "Nope. Just heard a little about the place."

The wind rattled the branches of a pine overhead. Some of the snow that had collected on those branches the night before slipped off and fell on Longarm, covering his shoulders and hitting his hat with a soft *thud*. He snorted in surprise, shook his head, brushed snow off his shoulders.

Nicole laughed.

It was a surprisingly light, pretty sound to come from a woman with such a hardened criminal history. Longarm looked over at her and saw that she was grinning again. He took his hat off and, without thinking about what he was doing, scooped up some of the snow that had landed on the Stetson's flat crown.

"Laugh at me, will you, woman?"

He tossed the snow at Nicole.

She laughed again as she ducked aside. Most of the snow missed her.

"I'm going to take pity on you, Mr. Parker, since you're a wounded man and all. Otherwise I'd be down off this horse and packing a nice snowball in my hands right about now."

Longarm grinned right back at her. "You couldn't hit me. I never yet saw a gal who could throw worth a darn."

"Oh, is that so?"

"Well, maybe one." He thought about Jessica Starbuck. "But she's way off down in Texas."

"We'll just see about that."

"Gonna throw snowballs at me, are you?"

"Not right now." She gave him an arch look. "But you'll never know when it's coming."

Longarm chuckled, finished brushing the snow off his hat and coat, and put the hat back on. He and Nicole had almost reached the town by now. The lay of the land led naturally toward the eastern end of the settlement, so that's where they went.

Longarm didn't see anybody on the street except the men near the bonfire at the far end. People were staying inside on this cold, snowy day. And the town was even less populated than it appeared to be from a distance. Fully half of the buildings were empty, with boarded-up doors and windows. Antelope wasn't a ghost town yet but it was well on its way to becoming one.

As they rode down the street, Longarm kept an eye out for a sign announcing the marshal's office. He didn't see one.

"Where is everybody? I want to find a doctor for you. Then I'll be on my way again."

"You're not going to wait out the storm here?"

"I can't. I'll buy a few supplies and then push on."

"You'll freeze to death if that blizzard catches you in the open again." Longarm made his voice harsh as he spoke.

"I survived last night, didn't I?"

"Might not be so lucky two nights in a row."

"I'll have to take that chance."

"Still running, eh?"

She looked over at him. Her mouth tightened. "I think what you mean to say is, thank you for saving my life."

Longarm shrugged. "I'm obliged to you, all right. That don't mean I think you ought to go gallivanting off into a Nevada snowstorm."

Nicole didn't say anything in response to his statement. Her attention, as well as Longarm's, was drawn by a door being opened in a building up ahead to their left. A tall man in a black suit stepped out onto the boardwalk. He wasn't wearing a hat. The wind ruffled his thick iron-gray hair. The lantern-jawed face bore a resemblance to Abraham Lincoln before old Honest Abe grew his beard. This man was even uglier than the rail-splitter from Illinois had been.

"Good Lord, what are you folks doing? Get on in here out of this godawful weather!"

Longarm looked past the man at the front window of the building. Gilt letters read UNDERTAKING PARLOR.

The man saw where Longarm was looking and laughed. "I won't say the place has got all the comforts of home, but at least you'll be out of the wind."

Earlier, as he was mounting up, Longarm had glanced at the hip of the horse he now rode. It bore an odd-shaped brand. Instead of letters or numbers a set of lines had been burned into the horse's hide to form the outline of a coffin. Longarm hadn't thought much about it at the time.

Now he found himself wondering if the men who'd tried to kill him and Nicole had any connection to the lantern-jawed man who had come from Antelope's undertaking parlor.

"Is there a doctor around here?"

"A doctor?" The man looked surprised by Nicole's question. "Are you hurt, ma'am? Or your friend here?"

"He's been shot. I patched him up the best I could, but he really needs a doctor to take a look at him."

The undertaker shook his head. "No, I'm sorry, we don't have a doctor here. Did have one but he left a while back. I know a little about such things, though. Help your friend inside and I'll do what I can for him."

Nicole nodded and was about to dismount when Longarm spoke. "What about a marshal? You got one of those in this settlement?"

"We certainly do. If you've been shot, I imagine you want to report it to the authorities. Come on in and while I'm looking at your wound, I'll send someone to fetch the marshal."

Warning bells were going off in the back of Longarm's mind. This fella sure wanted to get him and Nicole into the undertaking parlor. That eagerness put Longarm on edge.

"I'll talk to the marshal first. I'm all right for now."

"Nonsense. You don't want to take chances with a serious injury like a bullet wound." The man smiled. Didn't make him any less ugly. "I'd just as soon you didn't require my professional services any time soon, friend. The ground's already frozen. It's hard to dig a grave at this time of year."

Nicole swung down from her horse. "Stop arguing. It's cold out here. I'll help you in and then I'll go find the marshal."

If he agreed to that, he knew he'd never see her again. Instead of fetching the local badge, she would take off for the tall and uncut. In her circumstances a lawman was just about the last person she wanted to see.

Longarm lifted the reins and pulled the horse away as Nicole reached for the animal's halter. That turned the horse's hip toward the boardwalk and the man who stood there. His bony face tightened.

"The coffin brand!" He recognized it, all right.

"Damn it, Parker!" Nicole tried again to grab Longarm's horse. She hadn't put it all together yet, didn't realize the connection between the undertaker and the men who had bushwhacked them. Longarm tried to pull the horse around her so he could reach over and snag the butt of his Winchester where it stuck up from the saddle boot.

Before he could get the rifle, the door of the undertaking parlor opened again and a man stepped unsteadily onto the boardwalk. A bloodstained bandage was wrapped around his midsection.

"That's them, Uncle Vance! The ones who killed Teddy and Roy and Benjy!"

Longarm lunged for the Winchester, but a Colt appeared from under the man's black coat with a flicker of his ugly hand. The gun roared. Splinters flew as the bullet smashed the rifle's stock. Longarm had to jerk his hand back.

"That's enough." The ugly man thrust the barrel of his gun at Longarm and Nicole. The wounded hombre who'd come out of the building had drawn his gun and covered them, too. "Now the two of you are going to have to accept my hospitality. I insist."

Chapter 14

Nicole's eyes got big and darted back and forth like those of a trapped animal. With two guns pointing at her and Longarm at such close range, it was unlikely they could put up a fight and have any hope of winning. They'd been lucky during the battle at the bluff. That sort of luck didn't come calling often.

"Take it easy, Nicole. Don't do anything foolish."

Longarm's voice was low and urgent as he spoke to her. He had to get through to her before she panicked and started shooting.

The words seemed to do it. She took a deep breath and appeared to calm down although she was certainly still worried and more than a little frightened.

"That man . . . he's one of the gang that bushwhacked us. He's the fifth man."

Longarm had made that connection even before the wounded hombre stepped out of the undertaking parlor. The coffin brand on the horse he rode was enough for his brain to make that leap of logic.

"Yeah. The one who got away after all."

The man jerked his pistol up. The barrel shook a little

from the rage he felt. "You killed my brother and my friends, you son of a bitch!"

"Cass! Stop it!" The order came from the undertaker. "I don't want them dead until we know for sure who they are and what they're doing here."

"We're not *doing* anything." Nicole's voice was stronger now. "We were just looking for medical help for my friend here. He's been shot."

The young man called Cass sneered. "Yeah, by me or one of the boys with me."

"You fellas started the ball, old son," Longarm replied. "You shot at us. You were trying to kill us, first. No doubt about that."

His words didn't mean anything to Cass. The hate-filled sneer on his beard-stubbled face didn't go away. He was in his early twenties, short and stocky, but the evil stamped on his face was old.

The undertaker moved a step closer to the edge of the boardwalk and took over. "Get down from those horses and come inside. We're going to talk."

Longarm glanced over at Nicole and shrugged. "Not much we can do right now but go along with what he says." Surrendering went against the grain for him, but resisting would just get them killed. Better to wait for a more opportune time to make his move.

But sooner or later that time would come. Damn right it would.

He dismounted. So did Nicole. The undertaker nodded toward their mounts.

"Take care of the horses, Cass."

"I'm hurt." The complaint was a whine from Cass's mouth. "And it's cold out here. I don't even have a shirt on."

"Go put one on, then tend to the horses. Do as you're told." The undertaker's tone made it clear he wouldn't put up with any more arguing.

"Yeah, sure, Uncle Vance. Whatever you say."

"But before you go, take their guns. Make sure you don't overlook any weapons."

Cass holstered his Colt and came over to follow his uncle's orders. He took Longarm's revolver from Nicole and ran his hands over body to make sure she didn't have any other guns or knives. Enjoyed the search a little too much, too, the way Longarm saw it. Nicole kept her face tight and expressionless while Cass was pawing her.

His search of Longarm was more perfunctory. Didn't really matter because Longarm was unarmed at the moment. He thought about making a grab for the butt of Cass's gun but that was too risky with the undertaker closely watching him. The fella had said that he wanted Longarm and Nicole kept alive for the moment, but Longarm wasn't going to wager his life on that.

When the undertaker was satisfied that neither of them were packing iron anymore, he motioned with the gun in his hand for them to step up onto the boardwalk and come inside. Longarm and Nicole did so. The undertaker followed them and heeled the door shut behind him. It was warmer inside the building, with heat radiating from a cast-iron stove in the corner, but Longarm still felt a chill in his blood.

Probably the ruthless expression on the undertaker's ugly, lantern-jawed face was to blame for that.

"My name is Vance Roland. I'm the mayor of Antelope as well as the local undertaker."

"There ain't really a marshal in this town, is there?"

Vance Roland's smile didn't make him any prettier. "There used to be."

"Let me guess: He's dead and you've taken over."

"I suppose you could say I'm the acting marshal. My word is law in Antelope."

Longarm thought he saw the light of madness burning deep in Roland's eyes. That didn't mean the man was any less dangerous. Roland was lucid enough. He just didn't give a damn who he killed.

"We're sorry about what happened out on the trail. Those men attacked us. They would have killed us. We had no choice except to defend ourselves."

Nicole's words didn't seem to have any effect on Roland. The undertaker continued staring at Longarm. "Do I know you? Have we met before?"

Longarm shook his head. "Not that I recollect." He didn't add that he would remember a downright ugly pan like the one Roland sported.

"What's your name?"

"Custis Parker."

Roland looked at Nicole. "And you, lady?"

"I'm Nicole Gardner."

"An unmarried man and woman traveling together?" Roland chuckled and shook his head. "Not much for propriety, are you?"

Nicole tried to get through to him again. "Look, whatever you're doing here in Antelope is none of our business. We're just passing through this area. We're not looking for trouble."

"You killed one of my nephews and several other men who worked for me!"

"They didn't give us any choice!" Nicole's words came out in a wail of despair.

"What did you do with their bodies?"

The question seemed to take her by surprise. She blinked. "We . . . we buried them, of course."

"That's a lie. You left them for the wolves. You wouldn't waste time burying men who had tried to kill you, especially when the ground is as hard as it is this time of year."

Longarm moved his hand toward the inside of his coat. "I'm just taking out a cheroot. Easy on that trigger finger, Roland."

The undertaker nodded. "Slow and easy."

Longarm complied. Slowly and carefully he took a cheroot from the pocket of his shirt.

But while his hand was inside the sheepskin coat, the back of it pressed against the pocket holding the leather folder containing his badge and identification papers. If Roland found out he was a federal lawman, the chances of him and Nicole ever leaving Antelope alive would plummet right off a cliff. He had to figure out some way of hiding the folder.

Only thing, it wasn't there anymore.

Longarm was careful to keep the surprise off his face. He glanced at Nicole. She was the only one who could have taken his badge and bona fides. She must have found them when she came back the night before, while he was passed out.

And yet she had stayed with him anyway, knowing that he was a lawman. Knowing that he must have been pursuing her because of Harvey Kellogg's murder, if not for the other crimes she had committed before that. She could have ridden off again and left him to die. Hell, she had his gun and he was unconscious. She could have just put a bullet in his brain and ensured her safety that way.

But she hadn't done it.

Longarm lit the cheroot with a lucifer he snapped into life on his thumbnail. He drew in the smoke, blew it out in a near-perfect ring.

Roland smiled. "Very impressive. Are you trying to demonstrate to me how icy-nerved you are, Mr. Parker?"

"Nope. I just figure you got the upper hand here. You'll do whatever it is you want to do and I ain't sure we can stop you."

"You can't. Some of the people in Antelope tried to stand in my way. They failed. You saw the fire down at the other end of town as you rode in?"

Longarm couldn't help but frown. "The bonfire? Yeah."

Roland gave a soft laugh. "That is no ordinary bonfire, my friend. It's a funeral pyre for my enemies."

Longarm's jaw tightened. So those things he had seen being tossed into the flames . . .

"Oh my God." Nicole lifted her hands, pressed them to her mouth. She looked and sounded as sick as Longarm felt. "You mean . . . you mean you burned people . . ."

"Not alive. They were already dead."

"You . . . you monster!" Nicole bent at the waist, stumbled forward, gave a wretched moan. "I . . . I think I'm going to be sick."

She lurched forward again, her mouth wide open as if she were about to vomit all over Roland's boots.

Instead she tackled him, slamming into the man and driving him backward.

Chapter 15

Longarm had caught on to what Nicole was going to do before she made her move. She had seen and done too much to lose control that way just because of what Roland had told them. So Longarm was already moving when Nicole leaped at the undertaker.

She went underneath the gun so that the shot would go over her if Roland jerked the trigger. At the same time Longarm lunged forward, swung a fist, and batted Roland's gun aside. It blasted as his finger contracted. The bullet went wide and thudded into the wall.

Roland hadn't expected the attack. He was off-balance and went down hard on his back. Longarm lashed out with a booted foot and kicked the undertaker in the head. Roland went limp.

Longarm reached down, grabbed Nicole's arm, and jerked her to her feet. With his other hand he snatched up the gun Roland had dropped.

"Out the back—"

Longarm didn't have time to do more than start to urge Nicole out of the undertaking parlor before the front door burst open. Vance Roland's nephew Cass stood there. He screamed a curse as the gun in his hand came up.

"Ace! Spike! Get over here!"

The revolver blasted as Longarm shoved Nicole toward a door in the back of the room. He heard the slug rip past his ear. The Colt in his hand bucked as he snapped a shot at Cass. The man jerked back as splinters flew from the doorjamb next to his head.

That gave Longarm and Nicole time to reach the other door and slam through it. They found themselves in a back room where several empty coffins leaned against the wall. An embalming table sat in the middle of the room. Longarm knew what it was because he had once romanced a lady undertaker, of all things, back in Denver.

Another door led out the back of the building. Longarm heard Cass's heavy footsteps hurrying across the front room. He pointed at the other door and Nicole didn't waste any time getting there. She twisted the knob, flung the door open, and plunged out into an alley where snow had drifted about a foot deep.

They ran through the powdery white stuff, raising a cloud of it behind them. Cass was still yelling for help. His voice got louder as he reached the rear door of the undertaking parlor. His gun boomed twice, but both shots missed as Longarm and Nicole ran a zigzag pattern through the alley. Longarm twisted and threw another shot back at Cass. The move made pain stab through his wounded side, but he didn't pay any attention to it. He knew it was there, but it didn't mean anything.

Longarm's shot came close enough to make Cass duck back inside. Before he could look out again, Longarm and Nicole were gone. They had disappeared around the rear corner of a building that backed up to the other side of the alley.

They found themselves in a narrow, trash-littered passage headed toward Antelope's other main street. Longarm heard Cass yelling from somewhere behind them. Other men shouted questions back at him.

"Circle around! Cover all the alleys! Damn it, I think they killed Uncle Vance!"

Longarm knew good and well Vance Roland was still alive. He hadn't kicked the undertaker that hard. But Cass might have mistaken his uncle's unconsciousness for death.

Or maybe he was just trying to goad the other men into killing the two fugitives.

Loud, angry voices sounded up ahead. Roland's men were in the other street, too. Longarm spotted a flight of stairs leading up to a second-floor landing built onto the side of the building to their left. He grabbed Nicole's arm and steered her toward the steps.

"Up there!"

The words were pitched low enough so that the searchers wouldn't hear them. Longarm and Nicole began to climb the stairs. They moved fast, but tried not to make too much noise about it.

Longarm hoped the door at the top of the stairs wasn't locked.

It wasn't. Nicole opened it and they darted inside. Longarm heard men shouting at the mouth of the alley as he swung the door shut. If the searchers hadn't seen the door closing, there was a good chance that he and Nicole would be safe for a little while.

Roland's men would likely search the whole town, building by building. The respite wouldn't last long.

They found themselves in a corridor with a threadbare carpet runner on the floor. Half a dozen doors were on each side of the hallway. This had to be a hotel, though Longarm didn't know if it was still in use or not. The doors were all closed and no one was in the hall except the two of them.

Nicole's face was flushed from the cold and the exertion of their flight. She leaned close to Longarm and spoke in a whisper. "What do we do now?"

He tried the nearest of the doors. The knob turned. He

held the Colt ready as he opened the door and peered into the room.

Empty.

A bed and a ladderback chair were the only pieces of furniture in the room. Dust lay thick on them as well as the floor. Moth-eaten curtains hung over the window and let in some pale, watery light.

"This place used to be a hotel, but it don't look like anybody's stayed here for a long time."

"Do you think we'll be safe here?"

Longarm nodded. "For a while." He listened intently, but didn't hear any sounds coming from inside the old hotel. He reckoned that he and Nicole had it to themselves. For now. Until Roland's men started that intensive search.

A wave of weakness suddenly hit him. Nicole must have noticed it because she lifted the chair and placed it beside him.

"Sit down. I want to have a look at that wound in your side. You might've started it bleeding again."

Longarm didn't think that was the case, but he supposed it wouldn't do any harm to let Nicole check it. He sat down on the ladderback chair and opened his coat. Undid the buttons on his shirt as well and pulled the material back.

She looked at the bandages tied around his torso, ran her fingers lightly over them as well. "If the holes are bleeding, it hasn't soaked through yet. I guess you're all right."

She was kneeling in front of Longarm. The scarf she had worn around her face earlier had drooped enough by now so that he could see her without any trouble. Strands of blonde hair that had been tucked up under the slouch hat had escaped and now hung down, framing her face. Her eyes were a deep, sparkling blue like the waters of a high mountain lake in summertime.

"What did you do with my badge?"

A sharp intake of breath was Nicole's first response to

Longarm's question. Then she looked at him and tried to play ignorant.

"What badge?"

"The badge and identification papers in the leather folder you took from me last night. The ones that prove I'm a deputy United States marshal named Custis Long."

She shook her head. "I don't know what you're talking about. You told me your name is Parker and I assumed you're just a drifter—"

"Damn it, Nicole, there's no point in lying about it now! My badge is gone and you're the only one who could've taken it. I want to know where it is because if Roland and his men find it, they'll be even more eager to kill us both."

"I think they're already plenty willing to kill us because of what happened at the bluff. Not to mention the fact that you kicked Roland in the head and he doesn't seem like the sort of man to forget about that—or forgive it." She sighed. "But I suppose you're right about there not being any point in lying. I guess it's just a habit with me by now. That folder is in the saddlebags of my horse. The horse you were riding yesterday."

Longarm's face was grim as he nodded. "They'll likely find it, then. They'll be searching our gear soon if they haven't already."

"You didn't just happen to ride along and find me. You were looking for me." Her tone was accusatory.

"It was my job, Nicole. Or should I call you Nora or Nellie or one of the other names you've used to swindle hombres who were old enough to know better?"

She stood up, paced a few steps away, turned to glare at him. "Damn it, you don't know the whole story. You don't know what I've had to go through in my life, the obstacles I've had to overcome. Anyway, all those men got something in return for their money. Believe me, Marshal, they got value returned."

Her voice was as cold as the wind that blew outside and

rattled occasional flurries of snow against the window of the deserted hotel room.

"What about Harvey Kellogg? All he got was a bullet."

A change came over her face. She looked stricken. "I didn't kill Harvey. I've never killed anyone in my life except during that fight at the bluff, and I had no choice there."

"I thought we agreed that there wasn't any point in lying."

"I'm not lying, damn it! I didn't kill Harvey Kellogg!"

To tell the truth, Longarm had had a difficult time accepting the notion that the woman who had risked her neck to save his life was also a cold-blooded murderer. It wasn't impossible, but it just didn't seem to add up.

The question had to be asked anyway. "If you didn't kill him, who did?"

Nicole gave a bleak laugh as if she knew that no one would believe her.

"That's easy. Harvey's secretary murdered him. Miles Ambrose killed Harvey Kellogg."

Chapter 16

He looked at her for a long moment. She didn't flinch and he didn't see any sign on her face that she was doing anything but telling the truth.

"Why would Ambrose kill Kellogg?"

"I have no idea. Maybe he was stealing and Harvey found out about it. Maybe they had some sort of argument over something else. All I know is that I heard a couple of shots, and when I came into Harvey's study, I found Ambrose standing over him with that gun in his hand. Ambrose took a shot at me, too, but missed."

"What did you do then?"

"I struggled with him. I wanted to get the gun away from him."

"How come you didn't just turn and run?"

She gave him a scornful look. "If I'd done that, he would have shot me in the back. I knew fighting was the only chance I had. I thought I could take the gun away from that little weasel and I was right. It went off again just as I pulled it out of his hand. That one hit the window."

Everything she had told him jibed with Longarm's memories of what had happened two nights earlier. Two shots together, then another, then a fourth shot, which broke

95

out the window in Harvey Kellogg's study. Longarm had been outside the house. He hadn't been able to see who had actually been holding the gun when it went off.

Except for the fifth and final shot.

"You tried to ventilate me when I yelled through the window for you to hold it, right after you walloped Ambrose with that paperweight."

"That was you? Somehow, I'm not surprised. But I didn't know who you were. I had no idea you were a lawman. For God's sake, I had just come in and found my fiancé murdered, and the man who killed him was trying to kill me, too! I panicked. You yelled at me and I shot at you. It was just an instinctive reaction."

"Like running away instead of staying and explaining what happened?"

"Yes!" She clasped her hands together in front of her. "I know it was foolish. I should have stayed and explained. But . . . I have a habit of not trusting the law."

"Maybe because you've been breaking it for a long time."

Nicole shook her head. "I won't argue about that with you. I've made my choices and done what I had to do. But I'm not a killer. I didn't shoot Harvey. But after I lost my head and ran away, I knew that everyone would blame me for it anyway. Miles Ambrose is cunning and he never liked me to start with. I knew he would twist everything around and make it look like I was guilty. And that's exactly what he did, isn't it?"

Longarm shrugged. "I looked through that window, saw Kellogg dead, saw you with the gun in your hand. It wasn't such a wild guess to figure that you shot him."

"Except that I didn't."

"All I've got to prove that is your word."

Her chin tilted up in defiance. "That's all I have to offer."

For a moment they stayed there like that, with their eyes locked together. Then Longarm shook his head. "We can hash it all out later. Right now I reckon we've got more important things to worry about."

"Like Roland and his men hunting us?" Nicole crossed her arms over her chest and gave a stubborn shake of her head. "No. That's not more important. Not to me. I don't have much in the way of self-respect, Marshal. That's been gone for a long time. But I *know* that no matter what else I might be, I'm not a killer." Her voice softened somewhat. "And God help me, for some reason it's important to me that you know it, too."

Longarm stood up and moved closer to her. He put out a hand, rested it lightly on her shoulder. "Why'd you really come back last night?"

"I told you. Because I'm a damned fool. Because . . . I didn't want you to die."

"And after you found out I'm a lawman?"

"I still didn't want you to die. This may come as a surprise to you, Marshal—it did to me—but I still have a conscience. And I didn't think I could live with your death weighing on it for the rest of my life."

Longarm smiled. "You know what? I reckon I believe you."

A look of relief washed over her face. She moved closer to him, suddenly rested her head against his chest. That made the hat fall off her head, and the rest of her hair spilled around her face.

"Thank God. I don't know why it's so important to me, but it is."

Longarm slipped his left arm around her waist and drew her tighter against him. Raised his right hand and used it to stroke her hair. They stood that way for several moments in the chilly, deserted, dusty hotel room.

Finally Nicole lifted her head to look up at him. "What about Miles Ambrose? What are we going to do about that whole mess?"

"First of all, we've got to get out of Antelope alive. I

97

don't reckon Roland and his boys will make that very easy."

"No, but if we do . . . are you going to take me back to Virginia City?"

"I pretty much have to. But it'll be your word against Ambrose's and I plan to see to it that he has to answer some mighty hard questions. There's an old hymn that says further along we'll know more about it. That's how I figure we'll deal with that problem. Take it as it comes and get to the truth."

He didn't say anything about the other charges Nicole would face in connection with the cases that had put him on her trail to start with. Even if he could prove that she hadn't killed Harvey Kellogg, she could still wind up behind bars.

But that was better than walking up thirteen steps to the gallows. Anyway, they might not live long enough to worry about it. Not if that crazy undertaker and his gang of gunmen caught up to them.

Longarm pushed that thought away as Nicole rested her head against his chest again. His shirt was still open from her checking his bandages and he felt the warmth of her breath on his skin. Despite the stolen man's clothing she wore, he could feel the lithe curves of her body molded against him as well. Her breasts rose and fell harder as the rate of her breathing increased.

She had to be feeling some of the same things he was feeling: desperation, loneliness, fear . . . powerful emotions. They had been thrown together and a natural chemistry had ignited between them. Nothing might have come of it under normal circumstances . . . but these were far from normal circumstances. The danger they were in heightened every sensation, filled every breath, every touch, with urgency. Nicole shuddered against him and a soft moan escaped her throat.

"Marshal Long . . ."

"Custis." He put a couple of fingers under her chin, tipped it up so he could look into those incredibly blue eyes. "Call me Custis."

She didn't call him anything. She kissed him instead.

Longarm returned the kiss with the same insistent heat that flowed into him from Nicole's lips. Her mouth opened in invitation and he plundered it with his tongue. His hand moved down to the soft mounds of her breasts, cupped them, and squeezed them in turn. She moaned again. Her hand rubbed hard against his groin.

After what seemed like an eternity she pulled her lips away from his. "You're hurt. You'll break open those wounds."

"Not if we're careful."

A soft laugh came from her. "I'm not sure I can *be* careful right now, Custis. But I'll try."

The bedspread was dusty. Neither of them cared. Longarm sprawled back on it and Nicole went to work on his belt and the buttons of his trousers. She got them loose and pulled them down along with the bottoms of his long underwear. His erect manhood sprang free from its confinement and jutted up from his groin, a long, thick pole of male flesh throbbing with readiness. With an expression of awe on her face, Nicole wrapped her hands around his shaft as best she could. For a moment she ran her palms up and down it in a maddeningly sensual caress.

Then she stood up and began tugging at her own belt, her movements urgent almost to the point of being frantic.

She lowered her trousers and stepped out of them. Gooseflesh stood out on her creamy thighs as she climbed onto the bed and straddled Longarm's hips. He reached up, stroked the triangle of fair hair that covered her mound. His finger found her opening and slipped inside. She was already wet. Her mouth formed an "O" of pleasure as he explored her with a second finger.

When he took them out, she grasped his erection and

guided the tip of it to its goal. She rubbed the head back and forth along the damp folds until it was good and slick with a commingling of her juices and his. Then she began to lower herself onto him, spreading wide to accept him, engulfing him with her heat.

Her eyes closed in ecstasy as she slowly sheathed every inch of him inside her. Longarm watched her. At that moment, despite the man's clothing and the tangled hair, she was as beautiful a woman as he had ever seen in his life. Sensations such as she had never experienced before transfixed her, gave her an almost angelic glow. The chill in the room disappeared. It couldn't stand up to the fierce heat that the two of them were generating between them.

Nicole began to pump her hips when she hit bottom. Longarm's hips moved as he met her thrusts with his own. She leaned forward and cupped her hands around his face.

"Lie still, darling. Let me do the work."

Longarm obliged her. She was mighty good at what she was doing. Even though her movements were slow and deliberate, his passion built up to a white-hot crescendo in no time at all. Or what seemed like no time. To tell the truth, time no longer had much meaning for Longarm. Nothing existed but him and her and the exquisite connection between them.

His hands went under her shirt, found her breasts. He stroked the hard nipples with his thumbs and gently kneaded the soft flesh around them. She sighed and continued riding him. Her eyes were still closed. She began to pant with desire as her movements became faster.

Longarm felt his climax boiling up, and when shudders of culmination rippled through her he let go, too. He thrust deep inside her, as deep as he could go, and emptied himself into her. Spasm after throbbing spasm filled her to overflowing with his seed. Their shared climax seemed to last forever.

When it was finally over, she slumped down against his

chest. He felt the hard pounding of her heart and knew that his was galloping, too. His arms went around her and held as they tried to catch their breath. With one hand he massaged the muscles of her neck.

Suddenly she lifted her head. "Oh my God. I shouldn't be laying on you like this. I'm going to hurt you . . ."

Longarm chuckled. "I'm fine. Not even a twinge. You did such a good job of bandaging up those bullet holes I reckon I could even go again if you'll give me a minute or two."

"Oh, really?" She pushed herself up with her arms and grinned down at him. "I might just take you up on that—"

A man's voice echoed from somewhere downstairs in the abandoned hotel. He called out to a companion and another man's voice answered him. Longarm and Nicole both stiffened. Footsteps sounded down below. Echoed hollowly in empty rooms.

"They're here." Nicole's voice was a tiny whisper.

"Yeah." Longarm started to ease out from under her. "We'll get the drop on them and take their guns—"

The plan was a long shot, but it might have worked if they'd gotten a chance to try it.

But at that moment the old bed, strained by their weight, gave way underneath them with a splintering of broken slats and dumped them on the floor with a heavy crash.

Chapter 17

The echoes of that crash still filled the room when shouts of alarm came from below. Longarm fought his way free of the debris from the broken bed, lunged to his feet, yanked his trousers up. He had put the gun he'd taken from Cass in the holster where his own Colt normally rode. He filled his hand with the iron now, motioned sharply to Nicole as she scrambled out of the bed's wreckage.

"Stay down!"

She reached under the mattress and pulled out a broken slat with a jagged end. It could be used as either a club or a makeshift spear. "The hell with that!" A determined expression came over her face as she stood up. She was ready to do battle.

But as she stood there bare-legged with the tails of the man's shirt almost but not quite covering her naked lower half, Longarm thought she was just about the unlikeliest-looking Amazon he had ever seen.

That was all he had time for before heavy footsteps thudded down the hall.

Nicole sprang over to stand where the door would hide her when it was opened. Longarm moved the other way.

Another shout in the hall. "That racket came from in here!"

"Be careful! That son of a bitch took Cass's gun!"

A shoulder slammed against the door and knocked it open. Longarm saw Nicole's eyes widen in shock as the door came crashing back against her. He feinted to draw the gunman's fire. The gun in his hand had only two or maybe three rounds left in it and he didn't want to waste them.

He didn't have to use a bullet on the first man through the door. Nicole recovered quickly and lunged at him from behind, ramming the jagged end of the broken slat into his back. The man howled in pain, started to twist toward her. Longarm struck then. He reversed the gun in his hand and used the butt to clout the man in the head. The hombre wore a tall hat with a Montana pinch. It cushioned the blow some but not enough to keep him from being driven to his knees. Longarm hit him again and sent the man slumping senseless to the floor.

He scooped up the pistol the man had dropped. More footsteps pounded along the hall and a second man came in shooting.

Longarm had already dropped to his belly. The bullets went over him and shattered the glass in the room's single window. Longarm fired upward at a steep angle, which sent a slug tearing through the second gunman's shoulder. The man screamed and spun around. Nicole had grabbed up another bed slat. She broke it over the man's head. He collapsed.

Seemed like there were only two of them. Nobody else yelled or stomped around in the hotel. But Longarm was damned sure these two weren't the only men Vance Roland had looking for him and Nicole. The shots and the hollering would draw the other searchers in a hurry.

"Get your pants on. We better light a shuck out of here while we still can."

Nicole yanked the stolen trousers on and then thrust out a hand. "Give me a gun!"

Longarm was already reloading both pistols. When he had thumbed fresh cartridges into the empty chambers, he passed one of the guns to Nicole. Both Colts had six in the wheel. That extra shot might come in handy.

Longarm led the way, Easing along the corridor and staying close to the wall. Nicole followed close behind him. He didn't head for the outside stairs that had brought them into this place. Instead he found the main staircase, which led down into the dusty, deserted lobby.

One of the double doors that formed the hotel's main entrance stood open. Boards that had been nailed across it had been wrenched off and tossed on the porch outside; Longarm saw them from inside the lobby. The big front windows were boarded up, too, so he couldn't see through them. He held the gun ready, edged toward the open door.

The hotel fronted on the other street instead of the one where the undertaking parlor was located. Directly across this street from the hotel were a squatty log building and a barn. Faded signs on them read SNYDER'S BLACKSMITH SHOP and LIVERY STABLE. Chances were that Snyder, whoever he was, owned the stable, too. The doors on the front of the blacksmith shop were closed, but smoke crawled from a chimney that rose at the rear of the building.

Longarm nodded toward the blacksmith shop. "We'll try to make it over there. Maybe the smithy will help us. Even if he won't, the place has nice sturdy walls. We can fort up there." He glanced over at Nicole. "We'll go fast. Once we start, don't stop running no matter what happens. Don't stop until you're inside again."

"Custis . . ."

Whatever she'd started to say she didn't finish. She just took a deep breath and gave him a curt nod.

Both of them knew the time for talking was over.

They exploded out of the hotel, bounded across the porch, leaped to the street, and ran toward the blacksmith shop. Snow flew around their legs, kicked up by their feet.

"Shit, there they go! Down here! Damn it, they're headin' for Snyder's!"

Guns began to bang.

Longarm didn't slow down and neither did Nicole.

Bullets plowed into the snow around them. Screamed through the air near their heads. But none of the slugs found the mark. Longarm and Nicole neared the doors of the blacksmith shop.

"If they're locked, go around the back!"

Longarm hoped Nicole heard what he told her. She was a little behind him and he didn't look back over his shoulder. But he knew she was still there because he could hear the sound of her breathing, made heavy by the exertion of their sprint.

One of the double doors on the front of the blacksmith shop swung open about a foot. A man with a bushy black beard peered out at Longarm and Nicole.

Then he slammed the door. Longarm heard the sound of a bar being dropped inside. He and Nicole were locked out. No shelter from the storm of hot lead.

"Around the back!"

He veered to the left, toward the narrow opening between the blacksmith shop and the livery stable. Nicole was right behind him as he ducked into the gap. Splinters flew as some of the bullets searching for them found the wall of the barn instead.

Longarm slowed to let Nicole catch up with him. He took hold of her arm and shoved her toward the far end of the passage.

"Keep going and don't look back!"

"Damn it, Custis—"

"Go!"

She ran. Longarm swung around the other way, back

toward the street. A couple of men ran around the corner of the blacksmith shop.

"Look out! There he is!"

They tried to bring their guns up. Longarm didn't give them the chance. His revolver was already leveled. It barked two fast shots. Both men were hit in the body and driven backward.

As he turned to run after Nicole, Longarm wondered just how many men Vance Roland had working for him. Slowly but surely he was whittling down the odds.

But being on the run like this, in a town where they seemed to have no friends and no allies willing to stand up to Roland and his gun wolves, that luck would run out sooner or later. Longarm knew that. No man could survive for long with every hand against him.

He reached the rear corner of the livery barn and looked around.

Nicole was gone.

Longarm's breath hissed between tightly clenched teeth. He saw her tracks in the snow. They led toward the edge of town, which wasn't far off. He ran in the same direction. A few shacks were nearby. She must have gone to ground in one of them.

The tracks led straight toward a run-down cabin with a hodgepodge of tar paper and tin nailed to the walls. But then they disappeared abruptly in a welter of disturbed snow. Looked like somebody had come along and kicked the snow every which way.

Like a struggle had taken place here.

But how could there have been time for that? Trading shots with the two gunnies between the blacksmith shop and the livery stable had taken only a minute or so. If somebody had grabbed Nicole, they would have had to move mighty fast in order to do so.

Longarm had no other explanation. Nicole was gone and there was no denying that.

Even though the tracks stopped short of the ramshackle cabin, Longarm's instincts told him to search there. He had only moments, maybe seconds, before more of Roland's men might find him. He ran toward the shack.

"Nicole! Nicole!"

She didn't respond to his low-voiced call. A set of leaning steps led up to a sagging porch. Longarm took them in a couple of bounds.

"Nicole!"

This time he heard a response. It was muffled and unintelligible as if somebody had clapped a hand over her mouth as she tried to shout.

Longarm lowered his shoulder and hit the door.

He tripped on something as he charged into the shack. His momentum took him down. But he managed to hang on to his gun.

"Go, Jamey, go! You know what to do!"

The voice was thick and muffled, too, although the words were understandable. Somebody leaped over Longarm and dashed outside, moving too fast for Longarm to get a good look in the dimness of the shack's interior.

But he saw Nicole on the other side of the room. A man stood behind her with his left arm around her waist. He held her tightly as she tried to struggle. His gloved right hand was pressed over her mouth, just as Longarm had supposed. Above his hand Nicole's eyes were wide with fear.

Longarm felt a shiver of horror go through him, too, as he looked up at Nicole and her captor from the warped planks of the floor. The shadows made it hard to see, but he could tell that the man wore a long duster.

And he had no face. Peering over Nicole's shoulder at Longarm was a blank expanse where a nose and mouth should have been. The only feature Longarm could see in that nothingness was a pair of eyes burning with a pale fire.

Chapter 18

"Don't shoot!" The faceless man took his hand away from Nicole's mouth and held it palm out toward Longarm as the big lawman tilted up the Colt's barrel. "I'm a friend!"

Longarm's eyes had begun to adjust to the dimness inside the shack. He could tell now that the man wore some sort of hood over his head that concealed everything except his eyes. The hood was an unpleasant reminder of some owlhoots Longarm had run into on a previous assignment. Those varmints had called themselves the Hell Riders, and Longarm's encounter with them had come too damned close to getting him killed.

"I've been trying to convince the lady that I'm on your side. I don't know who you are. But if Roland's gunmen are after you, we should be allies, not enemies."

Longarm held off pulling on the trigger. Not only was Nicole blocking any shot he had at the faceless man, but Longarm was curious about what the weird-looking hombre had to say.

"If you're a friend, how come you're wearing a mask?"

"I have my own reasons for that. But I promise you that I don't mean any harm to you or the lady."

Despite being muffled by the hood, the man's voice was

deep and powerful. It held the sounds of culture and education—two things probably in short supply here in this half-deserted mining town in the Nevada mountains.

Longarm got to his feet. He kept the revolver pointed in the general direction of Nicole and the masked man.

"Please close the door. Roland's men may arrive at any moment, and we don't want them looking in here and seeing you."

That much at least made sense . . . whether anything else in this crazy town did or not. Without taking his eyes off Nicole and the man who still held her, Longarm heeled the door closed.

The man let go of Nicole. "You can join your friend now."

She hurried across the room to Longarm. With his free hand he grasped her arm. "Are you all right?"

She gave him a shaky nod. "Yes. Whoever that . . . man . . . is, he didn't hurt me."

"I actually *am* a man under this garb, although I know it's hard to tell." The wry tone of the masked hombre's voice told Longarm that there might be a smile on his face. "I'm Thomas Heath. Dr. Thomas Heath."

"You're a sawbones?"

"Yes, I am." Heath lifted a hand and pointed at Longarm's side. "And from the looks of that blood soaking through to your shirt, friend, I'd think you could use my services right about now."

It was true that Longarm had started to feel a mite woozy during the past couple of minutes. All the running and fighting and falling had finally busted open those bullet holes in his side. They throbbed with a dull ache. He steeled himself not to give in to the pain.

"I ain't in the habit of letting fellas who wear masks go to poking around on me, old son. I don't—"

"Sshhh!" Heath made a sharp gesture with a gloved hand. "They're out there!"

Longarm started to turn toward the window, then stopped short. Heath might be trying to trick him.

The masked man must have read Longarm's mind. "It's not a trick. Listen!"

Longarm listened and heard voices. Loud, angry male voices. Heath took a step toward the window as if anxious. He stopped. Longarm was between him and the oilcloth-covered opening.

"Keep him covered." Longarm handed Nicole the gun. She took it and directed a determined expression at Heath.

Longarm turned to the window and moved the oilcloth aside a fraction of an inch, just enough to see out.

Two men stood about halfway between the shack and the rear of the blacksmith shop and livery stable. They were talking to a boy about eight or ten years old who wore a ragged coat and a cap that had seen better days. The snow was marked by boy-sized tracks that went everywhere as if he had run back and forth all over the open ground between the shack and the buildings. The youngster pointed toward a line of bare-limbed trees that marked the path of a creek twisting close to the settlement. The men turned and hurried in that direction.

"Is the lad all right?" Heath's voice was filled with worry.

"He's fine. He sent those gunnies on a wild-goose chase." Longarm let the oilcloth fall closed and looked back over his shoulder at the masked man. "But they're liable to be pretty unhappy when they realize he steered 'em wrong."

"By that time, Jamey will be safely hidden away somewhere."

"Custis, what's going on here?" Nicole sounded as confused and baffled as Longarm had felt until a moment earlier.

Glimmers of understanding were starting to break through to Longarm's brain. He nodded toward the masked figure. "The good doctor here sent the boy out to brush away your tracks after he grabbed you. Probably with a pine branch or something like that. But after I came over here to the shack anyway, he told the boy to run back and forth and leave a bunch of tracks, figuring that Roland's men wouldn't find be able to find ours among them. That about right, Doctor?"

The hooded head moved in a nod. "That's right."

"He knew Roland's men would ask the kid if he'd seen us so he told the kid to send them in the wrong direction. That was taking quite a chance."

"I know." Heath's voice was thick with worry now. "I know. But Jamey has lots of practice at lying low. All the honest people still left in Antelope do."

"What in blazes happened here?"

"Before I explain, are you convinced now that I'm a friend, that I mean you no harm?"

Longarm took the revolver back from Nicole and holstered it. "I reckon I am."

"Would you like some coffee?" Heath gestured toward the stove. It had a hard time putting out enough warmth to keep up with the chilly wind whistling through cracks and gaps in the shack's walls. "There's still some in the pot."

Longarm nodded. "Sounds mighty good. We're obliged."

The door opened and the boy came in as Heath went over to the stove. "Did I do a good job, Doc?"

"You certainly did, Jamey." Heath's voice was expressive enough to convey the look of approval that was bound to be on his face. "You'd better run along, though, and avoid Roland's men for a while."

"All right." The boy looked up at Nicole. "You're pretty."

She looked like the compliment surprised her. She had to know she was attractive, so it must have been the timing of it. And the circumstances in which they found themselves.

"Thank you . . . Jamey, is it?"

"Yeah, that's my name." The boy switched his gaze to Longarm. "And you're tall, mister."

112

Longarm chuckled. "What, I ain't pretty, too?"

"Not hardly. So long."

Longarm shook his head and grinned as the youngster opened the door, peered around outside for a second, and then hurried out of the shack. A glance out the window told Longarm that Jamey was headed for some of the other shacks on the edge of the settlement.

"I reckon he ain't your boy?"

Heath brought tin cups of coffee to Longarm and Nicole. "No, Jamey's an orphan. His father was a miner before the mines hereabouts began to play out, and his mother worked as a cook in the hotel. His father was killed in a cave-in. Six months later a sudden fever took his mother. After that the town sort of adopted him, I suppose you could say. He helps me out sometimes." The masked man sighed. "He's the only one who still comes to visit me."

"You'd think that a sawbones would have plenty of patients."

"There was a time I did." Heath waved a hand in dismissal of that subject. "But there are more important things to talk about. Who are you and what brings you to Antelope?"

Longarm didn't see any point in lying. "Deputy U.S. Marshal Custis Long. The lady is Miss Nicole Gardner." Might as well use that name for her as any.

Heath stiffened. "You're a lawman? You've been sent here to deal with Roland and his gang?"

"No, it was just bad luck that brought us here." Likewise, Longarm didn't see any need to go into detail about his pursuit of Nicole. "We had a run-in out on the trail with some hombres who turned out to be a couple of Roland's nephews and some other gunnies. They bushwhacked us. We did four of 'em in but the fifth man got away. When we got here to Antelope, we found out that he was Cass Roland. He'd told his uncle all about us."

"Cass Roland is the scum of the earth just like the rest

113

of them." Dr. Thomas Heath's voice seemed to have a naturally gentle quality to it most of the time, but it hardened when he spoke about Cass Roland and the other gun wolves who had moved into Antelope and taken over the settlement. "I'm not surprised that he and his companions attacked you. They've been responsible for dozens of murders and robberies in the six months they've been here."

"I reckon they killed whatever law you had here."

Heath nodded. "Marshal Jackson. He was gunned down. Shot in the back. But that wasn't until we'd all started to realize just what sort of vipers we had welcomed into our midst."

Longarm had been warming his hands on the coffee cup. Now he took a sip of the strong black brew and felt its bracing effect. "You didn't know how bad Roland really was when he got here?"

Heath's shoulders rose and fell in the duster. "We had no way of knowing. He just seemed like any other businessman when he arrived and set up his undertaking parlor. He had his nephews with him, half a dozen of them. Roland said they were his helpers." The masked man picked up a chair and moved it toward Nicole. "I hate to see you standing, Miss Gardner. Won't you please sit down?"

Tentatively Nicole took a seat. "Thank you. This coffee is good. But how do you—"

Heath chuckled at the way she stopped short in her question. He finished it for her. "How do I drink with this hood over my head? I don't wear it all the time. Just when there are people around."

Longarm didn't care about that. He already had a pretty good idea why Heath had donned the mask. "What about Roland and his bunch?"

"Antelope was already a dying town when they arrived. We were actually glad that someone wanted to move here. People had been moving out ever since the mines began to close. And we needed an undertaker." Heath shook his head. "We needed one more than ever because people began to die. Hardly a week went by without someone in the vicinity being robbed and usually killed. More hard cases rode in and stayed at Roland's place. After a while we began to realize that he and the others were responsible for all the violence that had begun to plague the area. Marshal Jackson confronted Roland about it, but of course Roland denied everything. It was that same night the marshal was murdered."

"After that Roland didn't bother hiding what he was doing, I expect."

"That's right, Marshal Long. He declared himself the mayor and acting marshal and made it clear that he and his gang were now in charge in Antelope. And anyone who didn't like it was risking their lives to speak up in opposition." A bitter tone came into Heath's voice. "We found that out shortly thereafter when a couple of men who had challenged Roland's authority were beaten to death."

"Yeah, I've seen it before. A gang of owlhoots comes in and trees a town, runs roughshod over folks until they're too afraid to fight back anymore. How come you didn't send somebody to Virginia City to fetch some real law?"

"We tried. We sent two men. Roland's men brought their bodies back and dumped them in the middle of Main Street. They'd been shot full of holes. After that . . . well, we didn't try anymore."

Longarm understood. No one else had been willing to risk their lives. It was easier to just lie low and hope that Roland and his men would leave them alone. That the outlaws would pick somebody else to rob and kill.

What those folks didn't understand was that sooner or later varmints like that would come for them, too. Evil never died out of its own accord. It just grew and grew until somebody put a stop to it.

Usually with hot lead.

After a moment of silence Heath spoke again. "If you

can hide out here until nightfall, you might be able to get away then. You could steal some horses and try to get over the mountains."

Longarm listened to the wind blowing outside. It had gotten stronger. He shook his head.

"No, it's gonna come another storm. The snow will be too deep in the passes for us to get through. We'd get caught out there somewhere and freeze to death."

"Well, you can stay here, of course." Heath gave a hollow laugh. "If Roland's men find you here, they'll kill us all. But I don't really care. It's not as if I have a great deal to live for."

"You might want to think about that some more, old son."

"Why?"

Longarm drank the last of his coffee and set the empty cup on the table. "Because I don't intend to just sit and wait for those bastards to come and kill me."

"What else can you do?"

"Kill them first."

Chapter 19

Slowly Heath sat down at the table across from Nicole. "Fight back? You mean you're going to fight back against Roland and his men?"

"Somebody's got to." Longarm's reply was blunt. "Somebody should have before now. Good Lord, how many men does he have working for him?"

"I . . . I'm not sure. Fifteen? Twenty?"

"We've already killed some of them. He probably don't have more than a dozen men left."

"But they're all gunfighters. Vicious killers." Heath gave that humorless laugh again. "I know you must be really good with your gun, too, Marshal. Otherwise you wouldn't have been able to take down four out of the five men who jumped you on the trail."

Longarm nodded toward Nicole. "I didn't do it by myself. The lady can handle a gun, too."

She shrugged and smiled ruefully.

"Even so, the two of you can't hope to survive a battle with a dozen outlaws."

"How many folks are left here in Antelope? The honest ones, I mean."

"Eighty or ninety, I'd say. Perhaps as many as a hundred."

"So you've got Roland and his bunch outnumbered seven or eight to one."

Heath shook his head. "A lot of the citizens are women and children. With all due respect to Miss Gardner, you can't expect women and children to fight outlaws."

"Maybe not. But I'll bet the able-bodied men still outnumber Roland's gang by quite a bit. If you'd all act together—"

"People are afraid."

"You think the fellas who dressed up like Indians and tossed those crates of tea into Boston Harbor weren't afraid? You reckon those three hundred Spartan hombres at Thermopylae didn't wish they could just lay down their spears and shields and go home?"

Heath's head came up in surprise. "You're an educated man, Marshal."

"I've read a book or two in my time. But most of what I've learned has come from just living. One thing I've learned is that if something's worth having it's worth fighting for."

"Worth dying for?"

"If it comes down to that."

"I'm not sure this town is worth it." The hooded figure pushed up from the chair. "But my life isn't worth much, either. I'll join your campaign, Marshal. Just tell me what to do."

"Do you have a gun?"

"I have a rifle—a Winchester. I used to use it occasionally for hunting."

Longarm jerked his head in a nod. "Load it. You're liable to need it."

Heath took the rifle from a long trunk next to the sagging bed. He got a box of .44–40 shells from a crooked shelf and thumbed the rounds into the Winchester's loading gate until the magazine was full.

"Work the lever so you can put one more in."

Heath did as Longarm said. "You really think I'll need that extra round?"

"Better to have it and not need it than—"

Heath held up a gloved hand to stop him. "I know the rest of it." He put the box of cartridges in the pocket of his duster. "Now what, Marshal?"

Longarm edged aside the oilcloth window covering just enough to look out. The snow had started falling again. Even though the hour was only mid-afternoon, the sky had darkened so that it looked like dusk.

"Can you move around town without attracting too much attention?"

"Yes. I have plenty of experience avoiding Roland's men. Avoiding everyone, actually."

"Can you think of maybe a dozen fellas you trust, men who can keep their wits about them?"

"You mean men who won't panic in a fight?"

Longarm nodded. "That's exactly what I mean."

Heath thought it over, then gave a nod of his own. "I suppose so."

"Go talk to 'em. Tell them to load their guns and get ready for all hell to break loose. Can you do that?"

"I can try. But there's one problem. I don't know if they'll listen to me. I . . . don't have a very good reputation in this town anymore."

"Why's that?"

Heath gestured vaguely toward the hood he wore over his head. "People don't like to have anything to do with a . . . a monster."

Nicole looked surprised. "You're not a monster. You're just a man."

"I appreciate the sentiment, ma'am, but you haven't seen what's under here." Heath's voice had that wry sound again.

119

"I don't care. I'll admit I was frightened of you at first when I didn't know who you were. But you seem like a gentleman and for goodness' sake, you're a doctor—"

"I *was* a doctor; that would be more accurate. I haven't practiced medicine since that cave-in . . . and the fire that came after it . . ."

Longarm reined in the impatience he felt. "I'm sorry to hear about that, Doc, but we got to deal with Roland and his boys right now. See if you can round up those men like we talked about and tell them to meet here as soon as it's good and dark."

"All right, Marshal. I'll do my best. What are you and Miss Gardner going to be doing in the meantime?"

"Figuring out a way to get Roland and all his men in one place. They've got to be together when we hit them. If they're spread out, it won't work."

"Yes, I see your point." Heath hefted the rifle and went to the door. "Good luck, Marshal."

"You're the one who's gonna need it right now."

Heath took a hat off a nail next to the door and crammed it on his head; it made him look even more bizarre. He nodded to Longarm and Nicole, opened the door, and slipped out into the growing blizzard. The wind slapped the door shut.

Nicole waited a moment to be sure Heath was gone, then spoke in a quiet voice. "What in the world is wrong with him? Why does he wear that hood?"

"It ain't just the hood. He had gloves on, too."

"Well . . . it is rather chilly in here."

"Yeah, but I reckon what he's really trying to do is cover up all his skin. Something happened to him. He wasn't always the way he is now. You heard him talk about that mine cave-in and the fire that came after it."

"He was burned!"

Longarm nodded. "That'd be my guess. He probably went down in the mine to help the folks who were hurt. The cave-in opened up a pocket of gas and something set it off. The sawbones got out alive but was burned so bad folks couldn't stand to look at him anymore. So he wears the hood and the gloves and that long duster to hide the scars."

"But that's terrible! If what you're saying is true, Custis, then it wasn't his fault. He was hurt while trying to help people. He shouldn't be punished for that."

"Nope, he shouldn't be. But when was the last time you noticed life being fair?"

Nicole had no reply for that.

Longarm went back to the window to check the weather. "Snow's coming down mighty thick now. Roland will have to call off the search for us. Any tracks we might've left are getting covered up by fresh snow. That'll help Heath get around without being spotted, too."

"Do you think all of Roland's men will go back to the undertaking parlor?"

"More than likely. But we're gonna make sure of that."

"How?"

Longarm smiled. "What's the one thing that gets folks' attention in a frontier settlement faster than anything else?"

Nicole shook her head. "I don't know."

"Fire."

She arched her eyebrows. "You're going to . . . ?"

"That's right. We're going to burn down part of Antelope."

Chapter 20

Nicole stared at Longarm. "How can you burn down just part of the town? Won't the fire spread?"

"Not in this blizzard. We'll pick one of the abandoned buildings that's not too close to anything else and set it on fire. Roland and his men will be like everybody else who lives out here on the frontier: Instinct will make 'em converge on the blaze before they realize that it can't spread. And then the group that Heath recruits will open up on them."

"Ambush them, you mean."

Longarm shrugged.

"That's murder."

"Well, if I had a troop of cavalry or a posse of marshals to work with, I'd probably give those outlaws a chance to surrender. But what we've got is a bunch of townsfolk that we can't count on. Some of them will miss with their first shot. Then it'll be a fight. We got to cut the odds down the best we can right from the start."

Nicole nodded. "I see your point. And I know you're right. What can I do to help?"

"Nothing right now. We just wait for Heath to get back and let us know he's got the men we need."

A thoughtful expression came over Nicole's face. "Dr. Heath's going to be gone for a while. We have some time to ourselves again, Custis."

Longarm had to grin. "These are even worse surroundings than that abandoned hotel room. And you know how that ended up."

Nicole got to her feet. "Come over here and sit down."

Longarm supposed it wouldn't hurt anything. He did as she said, taking the chair where she had been sitting.

She knelt in front of him and began unfastening the buttons of his trousers. "Are you sure you're up to this?"

He looked down at his side, where the bloodstain on his shirt was no longer spreading. "The bleeding seems to have stopped. I don't reckon what you've got in mind is gonna hurt me any worse than I already am."

"It's not going to hurt at all." She freed his already erect shaft and stroked her palms along its length. "In fact, it's going to feel wonderful."

Longarm didn't doubt that for a second. Nicole's blonde hair fell forward around her face as she leaned toward him and took the head of his stiff member in her mouth.

He sighed in pleasure and closed his eyes as she ran her tongue all around the crown. She held the shaft in both hands and continued to caress it as she licked and sucked and even bit lightly at the sensitive head. The tip of her tongue teased at the opening where Longarm's juices began to bead. Nicole stroked up with her hands, milking more of the moisture from him so that she could lap it up.

She lifted her head from his groin. "I love doing this." The whispered words sent an erotic charge rocketing through Longarm's veins. They were followed by an even more exciting sensation as Nicole opened her mouth wide and took in as much of him as she could. Her sucking took on an added urgency as if this intimate action she was performing caused her own passion and excitement to grow.

124

Longarm knew he couldn't withstand such exquisite torment for long. Nicole didn't seem to want him to delay his climax. Her eagerness was unmistakable. So Longarm buried his fingers in her thick blonde hair and surged into her mouth. She accepted him with ease and swallowed wantonly as he emptied himself into her. Her body bucked as a climax of her own rippled through her.

Spent, Longarm sagged back in the chair. Drew in a deep breath. Nicole's hands tightened to squeeze the last drops from him. When she had gotten all that she could get, she looked up at him and smiled.

"I wanted us to experience that together, Custis, before it was too late."

He slid his fingertips along her cheek and the line of her jaw, then cupped her chin. "Don't go to thinking like that. We're going to come through this just fine."

"Yes, but if we don't, it means a lot to me that we've been able to share these things. It means even more that you believe me about what happened up in Virginia City. You *do* believe me, don't you, Custis?"

Longarm nodded without hesitation. "Yeah. We've gone through enough together that I don't reckon you'd lie to me now. You didn't try to lie to me about any of the things you done before you took up with Kellogg."

She laughed as she tucked his now-limp member back in his trousers and began fastening the buttons again. "What point would there be in lying? Yes, I've swindled men in the past. Many times. If I have to answer to the law for that, then so be it. But I'm not a murderer, and I'm glad you believe me about that."

Longarm stood up and drew Nicole to her feet as well. He leaned down and kissed her, and wrapped his arms around her in a tight embrace. She returned both the kiss and the hug with equal fervor. When they broke the kiss, it was with great reluctance on both of their parts.

"We'll wait for the sawbones to get back, then fill him in

on the plan. Unless there's something else you'd like to do . . ."

Nicole shook her head. "No, I'm fine. For the first time in ages I really am fine."

Longarm believed her. He checked the coffeepot on the stove, found that there was still a little coffee in it. He poured it in their cups, then found a bag of Arbuckle's on a shelf and put some more on to boil, using water from a bucket beside the stove. It might turn out to be a long night. They would need the coffee.

Dr. Thomas Heath returned about an hour later. He came in, shook snow from his hat, and stomped it from his boots.

"It's bad out there. The snow's coming down so hard you can't see more than fifteen or twenty feet. If I didn't know my way around so well, I might have gotten lost and not even been able to find my way back here."

"Did you see any of Roland's men?"

"No. They've probably all gone back to the undertaking parlor. Is that where we're going to attack them?"

Longarm shook his head. "We're not going to let them fort up in there. Better to hit 'em while they're out in the open. You got men lined up?"

"Yes. Fourteen, in fact. That's two more than you asked for. We'll be taking on Roland's men on fairly even terms . . . other than the fact that they're outlaws and we're ordinary citizens."

"Ordinary citizens can accomplish a whole heap when they put their minds to it."

"How are you going to get Roland's men out into the open?"

Longarm explained his plan. Heath stiffened when Longarm mentioned starting a fire. Longarm didn't know if the reaction was caused by a natural worry about the possibility of burning the whole town to the ground or by memories of what had happened to the doctor to cause him to don a hood and gloves and hide himself away from everyone else in Antelope—except, apparently, from the boy Jamey. But when Longarm had finished going over the plan, Heath nodded.

"It might work. Taking them by surprise like that is our only real chance."

They drank more coffee and gnawed some biscuits, which Heath had left over from his breakfast that morning. The doctor had Longarm take his coat and shirt off so he could have a look at the wounds in the big lawman's side, something he had mentioned earlier but hadn't taken the time to do until now. Longarm grunted, but that was the only sign he gave of the pain as Heath worked the shirt loose from the dried blood.

Heath looked over at Nicole. "You said that you tended to these wounds earlier?"

"That's right. Did I do something wrong?"

"On the contrary. You did an excellent job. It's not your fault the marshal insisted on exerting himself and opened them again."

Actually some of those exertions sort of *had* been Nicole's fault. Longarm restrained a chuckle as that thought crossed his mind. He was just as much to blame as she was for the carrying-on they'd done.

"What did you use to clean them?"

"Whiskey."

Heath nodded. "That's effective but I have some carbolic acid. It's even better. I'll clean the wounds again and put some real dressings on them. I don't see any signs of infection so far. You're lucky, Marshal, to have a woman like Miss Gardner to take care of you."

Nicole laughed. "You just don't know how much trouble I can be, Doctor. Isn't that true, Marshal?"

"I wouldn't say that."

The truth was, he probably wouldn't be alive now if it hadn't been for Nicole. That thought weighed on his mind.

Assuming they lived through this trouble with Vance Roland and the crazy undertaker's gun crew—and that was a mighty big assumption, Longarm knew—he would have to take Nicole back to face justice for her crimes. That was his job. Even if she hadn't killed Harvey Kellogg—and Longarm intended to try to prove that—she was guilty of other things.

But the Good Book said for he who was without sin to cast the first stone—and Longarm knew damned good and well he had no business chunking rocks at anybody.

Packing a badge for Uncle Sam wasn't just a dangerous, low-paying job. Sometimes it was downright troublesome.

Longarm gritted his teeth when he felt the bite of the carbolic acid on the bullet holes in his side. Heath cleaned the dried blood away and poured a copious amount of the fiery stuff into the wounds. He covered them with cloth pads and tied those pads tightly in place with strips of actual bandage. Even with gloves on, his touch was deft. Longarm figured the man had been a fine doctor before tragedy had forced him to retreat from his profession.

"You should get rid of that bloody rag of a shirt. I think one of my shirts would fit you. It might be a little tight through the shoulders but you could manage."

"Thanks, Doc. I appreciate what you're doing for me."

"No thanks necessary. You're putting your life on the line, Marshal, for a town that I'm not sure deserves it. We all let Vance Roland and his killers come in here and take over."

"Like you said, you're just ordinary folks."

"But we didn't rise to the occasion. Not yet, anyway."

"Tonight you've got another chance."

That was true. A few minutes later, as Longarm finished putting on the borrowed shirt and shrugged back into his sheepskin coat, the men Heath had visited earlier began to arrive. They trudged up to the shack through the darkness and the snow and knocked softly on the door. Heath let them in one by one until more than a dozen people were crowded into the small shack.

He introduced the men to Longarm. Storekeepers, a clerk from the assay office, the local schoolteacher . . . not warriors, not by a long shot. But they were the only army Longarm had.

None of the names meant anything to him until Heath introduced a burly man with a tangled black beard. "This is Arlo Snyder."

Longarm thought the man's face looked vaguely familiar. "Snyder. From the blacksmith shop?"

Arlo Snyder grimaced and shuffled his feet. "That's right, mister. I'm the one who slammed my door in your face when Roland's men were chasin' you and the lady. I owe you both an apology. I just got scared when I saw them gunnies. I knew if I helped you, they'd kill me, too."

"Probably would've tried to, anyway."

"But I'll make it up to you." Snyder's big hands tightened on the rifle he had brought with him. "I'm a good fighter when I get my dander up. All I need is another chance."

"You'll get your chance." Longarm looked around at the group of men. "You all will. Now listen close, boys, and I'll tell you how we're gonna take your town back from Roland and the rest of those owlhoots."

Chapter 21

Longarm explained the plan. The men would fan out through the settlement and find positions where they could get good shots when the outlaws were drawn into the open by the burning building.

Dr. Heath suggested which building would be best suited for what Longarm had in mind. "You can set the old Kelleher Hardware Store on fire. It's empty, been abandoned for a couple of years. And there are vacant lots on both sides of it so there'll be less danger of the fire spreading." He told Longarm how to find the building.

"The way that snow's coming down there ain't much chance of the fire spreading anyway. It'll put out any sparks that blow toward the other buildings in town."

Heath nodded. "Yes, I think it's safe enough. When will we know it's time to strike?"

Longarm took the turnip watch out of his pocket and flipped it open. The watch was ticking along steadily as usual despite everything that had happened.

"I'll wait at least half an hour before starting the blaze at the old hardware store. That'll give you fellas time to get in position. You'll need to be patient and wait for Roland and his men to come out in the open. We think there's only about a dozen of them left, so make sure most of 'em are where you can get a clear shot before you start the ball rolling." Longarm looked around at the townsmen. "I know it may bother some of you to gun them down without any warning like that—"

One of the men interrupted him. "There ain't a one of us here who ain't lost friends or family to those polecats, Marshal. It's not gonna be that hard to pull the trigger."

Murmurs of agreement from the other men.

Longarm nodded. "All right. Spread out and wait for that building to go up in flames. Be careful. Pick your shots and make 'em count."

Grim nods came from the men. They began to file out of the doctor's shack.

When they were gone, Heath took a can from one of the shelves and held it out to Longarm. "You'll need something to start the fire. I've got a little coal oil here. If you break in the back door of the hardware store and pour this around inside, the whole place will burn."

Longarm heard the slight catch in Heath's voice every time the sawbones talked about fire. That made him more convinced than ever that his hunch about the reason for the hood and the gloves was correct.

"Doc, I'd be obliged to you if you'd stay here and look after Miss Gardner for me."

Nicole looked surprised. Judging by the way the doctor suddenly lifted his head, he probably did, too.

"I'm going with you, Custis," Nicole said.

Longarm shook his head. "Be better if you didn't. There's gonna be a lot of lead flying out there in a little while."

"More than there was out on the trail when Cass Roland and his friends ambushed us?"

"Might be. Probably will be."

Nicole gave a stubborn shake of her head. "I don't care. I'm coming with you."

"And I thought I would go, too. I can fight." Heath sounded as stubborn as Nicole looked.

"I don't know if that's a good idea, Doc. What with the fire and all."

Heath stiffened. "What are you talking about?" The tremor in his voice betrayed the depth of the emotions that had to be coursing through him.

"Sorry. I probably spoke out of turn there."

"You think you know what happened to me, is that it? You think you know why I am . . . the way I am?"

"I said I was sorry. It ain't none of my business—"

"No, it's certainly not. It's enough that I'm willing to help you."

Nicole moved closer to the doctor and put a hand on his arm. "Of course it is, Dr. Heath. We appreciate everything you've done. Don't we, Custis?"

"We darned sure do, old son."

Heath took a deep breath that caused the fabric of the hood to suck in where his mouth was. He pulled away from Nicole, went to the table, sat down, and let his gloved hands hang between his knees.

"We have some time. I suppose I could tell you the story."

"There ain't no need to do that."

Heath shook his head. "No, I want to. You should know what you might be getting into by trusting me." He paused for a second before continuing. "I mentioned the cave-in that took the life of Jamey's father. We all heard the rumble of falling rock even here in town and knew what had happened. I hurried up to the mine as fast as I could. Men were already down in the shaft trying to dig out the injured miners. I went down to help, to do what I could for the men who were hurt."

Nicole went over to him and touched his shoulder. "That was very noble of you."

Heath shook his head. "Not at all. It was just my duty.

133

Men were suffering and I was a doctor. But I'll admit . . . I was never very fond of being underground."

"You and me both, Doc. I never cared for that, neither."

Heath nodded as if he appreciated Longarm's words. "I got down to the level where the cave-in occurred and started doing what I could to help. Several men had been killed, crushed by the rocks, but others were just injured. They would have been all right if we could have gotten them out."

"But there was a gas pocket down there, right?"

"You *do* know something about mining, don't you, Marshal? Yes, gas began to leak into the shaft. One of the men smelled it and yelled a warning, told us to head for the elevator. But before we could flee, the gas reached the flame in one of the lanterns and ignited." Heath clasped his hands together tightly to keep them from shaking at the memories. "It was like hell down there. Suddenly flames were everywhere. Men shrieked as they burned. The men who were pinned by the rocks had no chance at all. They roasted right where they were."

"My God." Nicole's voice was a horrified whisper.

"I was the closest to the elevator but I didn't escape the flames, either. I was burned . . . my hands, my face . . . burned until it felt like the flesh was falling off my bones. My clothes were on fire. But I was still able to move. I . . . I left everyone else right where they were and stumbled to the elevator. I was able to throw the lever, which sent it up even though I screamed when my hands touched it. On the way to the surface I . . . I passed out. I was the only one who escaped. The men who had been trapped in the cave-in, the men who went down to rescue them . . . they all died."

"That wasn't your fault, Doc. You didn't cause the cave-in, you didn't have anything to do with that gas getting into the mine, and nobody could blame you for saving yourself."

"Ah, but they did. Perhaps it wasn't logical . . . but if you'd lost a loved one down there, a husband or a brother or a son, it would be only natural to feel some resentment toward the man who made it out. The *only* man who made it out. The man who left everyone else to die. If I'd just waited to send the elevator up—"

"Then likely you would've died, too."

"Perhaps that would have been better. The resentment felt by the people who were grieving, coupled with their equally natural horror at my injuries, meant that no one in Antelope wanted to have anything to do with me anymore. Well, no one except Jamey, anyway. The young are seldom as intolerant as their elders."

"Folks responded tonight when you went around looking for help."

Heath nodded. "But only because they hate Vance Roland and his gunmen even more than they despise me."

Nicole had pulled back a little while he was telling his story but she moved closer now. "You poor man . . ."

Heath's head came up. "Wait. You feel sorry for me, Miss Gardner. You want to comfort me. You're thinking about giving me a hug, I know. But before you do, you should know exactly who it is you're comforting." His hand lifted to the hood. "What it is—"

He jerked the mask off.

Longarm had to give Nicole credit. She didn't scream. Didn't even jerk back. She just stood there with her face frozen.

Longarm didn't flinch at the sight of Heath's ruined features because he had seen folks who had been badly burned before. He had come on the grisly leavings of more than one Indian raid where the slaughtered settlers had been left in their burning cabin. He knew what flames could do to a human body.

All the hair had been burned off Thomas Heath's head. A few tufts of it had come back in on his pink, scarred

135

scalp. His eyebrows and the rest of his hair seemed to be gone for good, though. His lips were an impossibly thin line, his nose a stub of what it had once been. His ears were mostly gone, too. Grotesque pink and white and gray scar tissue lay over everything. Heath was lucky not to have been blinded by the flames—if a man who had suffered the torments he obviously had could ever be called lucky.

"There, Miss Gardner. That's who you were about to hug. I won't blame you if you want to run screaming out into that blizzard."

Nicole took a deep breath. "No. Not at all." She stepped closer to Heath, leaned over, and put her arms around his shoulders. She hugged him, pressed her own cheek to his destroyed one. Longarm saw the doctor's eyes widen in amazement, then flare in anger.

He pulled away from Nicole and stood up. "I don't need your pity." He turned his back to her and Longarm. Tugged the hood back over his head and then jammed his hat down on top of it. He picked up the Winchester he had placed on the table earlier. "Let's go kill some outlaws."

"I can't talk the two of you into staying here?"

Heath shook his head. "I'm part of this."

Nicole nodded. "So am I."

Longarm hefted the can of coal oil and gave a nod of his own. He led the way as the three of them went out into the storm.

136

Chapter 22

Thomas Heath took the lead as they trudged away from the shack, since he knew his way around Antelope much better than Longarm did. On a night like this it would take someone who knew where he was going. The clouds cut off all light from the moon and stars, and the swirling snow made it even more difficult to see. Longarm, Heath, and Nicole stayed close together so they wouldn't get separated.

They hadn't gone very far when Heath stopped short and lifted his rifle. Longarm saw the doctor's alarmed reaction and reached for the holstered revolver on his left hip.

He relaxed a second later as he heard Heath's startled exclamation. "Jamey! What the devil are you doing out here, son?"

Longarm saw the boy then: a small dark shape in the curtains of white formed by the blowing snow.

"I was on my way to your place, Doc!" Jamey raised his voice to shout over the wind. "There's somethin' goin' on in town! I keep seein' men with guns!"

"That's all right, Jamey. They're friends of ours. Go on to my shack and wait for me there."

"Where are you goin'? Can't I come with you? Who's those folks with you?"

The youngster was full of questions. Heath didn't answer them, at least not fully. "You remember Marshal Long and Miss Gardner? We have some important work to do. Please, Jamey, wait for me at the shack."

"Are you sure, Doc?"

"Yes, I'm sure."

The boy gave a grudging sigh. "Well, all right. It's really snowin', ain't it?"

"Yes. It's a blizzard."

Jamey walked on toward the doctor's shack. Longarm watched him go. "Can he find his way there in this storm?"

"Jamey knows his way around Antelope just about as well as I do. I'm not surprised that he noticed those men getting into position for the ambush. Somehow he always knows what's going on."

Nicole asked a question that had already occurred to Longarm. "What if those were Roland's men Jamey saw? What if Roland's found out about our plan some way?"

Longarm provided the answer. "That's a chance we'll have to take. Come on, Doc. It's been more than a half hour. Snyder and the others should be ready by now, if they're ever going to be."

They reached one of Antelope's main streets a few minutes later. It was deserted but lights burned in several of the buildings, spreading a faint glow along the blocks. Heath pointed out a structure not far away.

"That's the old hardware store. You can circle behind it and get in, Marshal. Even if the back door is locked, you shouldn't have any trouble breaking it down. The building's not very sturdy."

Longarm nodded. He and Heath and Nicole stood at the corner of another building. He looked along the street and located the undertaking parlor. Roland's place was lit up brighter than any other building in town. Longarm saw shadows shifting against the glass of the front window as the men inside moved.

"The whole bunch is probably in there. Too bad we can't get at them like that. But when they see the flames, they'll come a-running. They won't be able to stop themselves." Longarm looked at Heath and Nicole and gave a curt nod. "The two of you stay here. This is as good a spot as any for you. When the shooting starts, pour as much lead as you can into those owlhoots."

"Where will you be, Custis?"

"I'll be around, don't worry about that."

Heath sounded a note of caution. "The wood in that building is old and dry, Marshal. The interior will go up like a tinderbox. You'd better get out quickly once you've set the fire."

"That's just what I plan to do."

Nicole put her arms around Longarm and gave him a quick but hard hug. "Be careful, Custis."

He returned the hug and promised that he would. Then he stuck his hand out to Heath.

"Thanks for all your help, Doc. For what it's worth I think the folks hereabouts have got it all wrong about you."

Heath took Longarm's hand in a firm grip. "It's worth a lot, Marshal. Thank you."

Carrying the can of coal oil, Longarm made his way toward the rear of the abandoned hardware store. There was enough light here along the street for him to be able to find his way despite the thick shroud of snowy darkness.

He didn't see anyone else, but that was a good thing. The riflemen recruited from among Antelope's honest citizens were well hidden as they waited for their chance to take back the town from Roland's gang.

Longarm padded through a foot-deep snowdrift along the side of the empty building. He reached the rear corner and turned to his left. The glow from the street didn't reach back here. He switched the coal oil from his left hand to his right and then used his left to feel his way along the wall. His feet bumped against some steps. It was a short flight to a landing where he found a door, but when he twisted the knob it failed to turn. He grasped it tightly, put his shoulder against the door, shoved. The jamb gave way with the sound of splintering wood.

Longarm shoved the door back and stepped into the stygian gloom of the building. He stumbled ahead with his empty hand held out in front of him, came to a wall, and felt along it until he came to another door. That one opened just fine. The hollow echo of his footsteps told him he had just entered a big, empty room. The main room of the store, more than likely. He unscrewed the cap on the can of coal oil. The reek of the stuff filled the air.

"Get him! Don't let him start that fire!"

The voice sent a shock of surprise through Longarm. *They were waiting for him!* He recognized the harsh tones of Vance Roland's voice. Somehow the undertaker knew about the plan to burn down the building.

That realization took only a fraction of a second to flash through Longarm's brain. As footsteps rushed at him, he whirled around, slinging as much of the coal oil out of the can as he could. The smell became even more overpowering. He flung the can blindly away into the darkness and reached under his coat for his gun. Maybe the spark from a shot would set off the coal oil.

He palmed the revolver from the holster, but before he could press the trigger something—or somebody—slammed into him from behind. He staggered but didn't go down. His left elbow drove backward into the belly of the man who had just hit him. At the same time he sensed someone in front of him and chopped at them with the gun in his other hand. The revolver thudded against something. A man groaned.

An arm went around Longarm's neck and tightened, cutting off his air supply. A hard-swung fist crashed into the side of his head.

"Don't let him shoot! Get his gun!"

140

That was Roland again. Longarm tried to bring the gun around to fire in the direction of the undertaker's voice, but a heavy weight clung to his arm, holding it down.

More hands grabbed him, shoved him off his feet, bore him to the floor. The gun was wrenched out of his hand. Booted feet thumped hard against his ribs, rolling him back and forth and breaking open the wounds in his side yet again. He reached up, grabbed somebody's leg, twisted and heaved. The owner of the leg went down with a startled yell. The floorboards shook under the impact of his landing.

Longarm got a hand inside his coat again, found a lucifer in his pocket. He brought it out even as more punches and kicks jolted him. Even though something had gone wrong with the plan, if he could just light the fire, the rapidly spreading flames would force Roland and the other outlaws to flee from the building. The townspeople could cut down at least some of them as they ran out of the burning hardware store. But first Longarm had to light the sulfur match and kindle the blaze . . .

He snapped the lucifer to life with his thumbnail. The sudden glare was blinding in the thick shadows. Longarm squinted against it, spotted a dark splash of coal oil on the floor about a yard away. The flash of fire might consume him, too, but he had to risk it. He got ready to toss the match toward the liquid.

A boot heel came down on his hand before he could do so, pinning it to the floor. His lips drew back from his teeth in pain. The man who had just stomped Longarm's hand reached down and plucked the burning match from the lawman's fingers. He lifted the lucifer and blew it out with a puff of breath. In that second the glare from the match illuminated the beard-stubbled face of Cass Roland, the undertaker's bloodthirsty nephew.

"Hold him down, boys. We got him, Uncle Vance. You want us to go ahead and kill him?"

Roland's answer came back without hesitation. "No.

141

Take him over to the undertaking parlor. I'm not finished with Marshal Long just yet."

So Roland knew he was a lawman. That didn't come as a big surprise to Longarm.

Once things started going to hell, they usually went all the way.

Chapter 23

Hands grabbed Longarm, jerked him to his feet. His hand still hurt where Cass Roland had stomped it and his side ached where he'd been shot. The warm stickiness he felt on his skin told him that the wounds were bleeding again. He hoped he had plenty of blood left. At the rate he was going, he would probably lose some more of it before the night was over.

His captors hustled him out of the hardware store, going out through the front door this time. With a man on either side of him holding his arms in a tight grip and several more around him, he was forced up the street to the undertaking parlor. He wondered if Nicole and Heath were able to see that he was a prisoner. What would happen to the plan now? Obviously the townspeople weren't going to be able to catch Roland's gang out in the open.

When they reached the undertaking parlor, one of the men opened the door and the two hombres holding Longarm shoved him through it. They let him go and he stumbled and nearly fell. As he caught his balance, he saw that he had almost tripped over something.

When he looked down at the floor, he saw the unseeing eyes of Arlo Snyder staring back up at him. The burly, bearded owner of the blacksmith shop and livery stable was dead. Blood stained the front of his coat and shirt. It had flowed from the gaping wound in the man's throat, under the black, jutting beard.

Longarm figured he was looking at the reason Vance Roland knew about the plan that had been hatched in Dr. Heath's shack.

The undertaker confirmed that as he came into the room behind Longarm. Roland gave a harsh laugh. "Poor Arlo couldn't talk fast enough when we showed him the knife and told him what would happen to him if he didn't tell us what was going on. Some of my men caught him skulking around with a rifle and knew that something had to be wrong. Despite his size Arlo Snyder was a coward through and through, like most of the other people in this town."

"I reckon he must've told you I'm a lawman, too. But talking didn't save his life, did it?"

"No, Marshal, it didn't. But it allowed us to stop you from carrying out your foolish plan." Roland laughed again. "Arlo looked so disappointed when I told Cass to cut his throat anyway."

Cass had followed his uncle into the room. He grinned. "Sure made a funny gurglin' sound when I pulled the knife across his neck, too."

Longarm kept his face expressionless, didn't show the revulsion he felt toward these hardened killers. He hadn't had much use for Arlo Snyder, but no man deserved to die like that.

About a dozen men were now crowded into the room. Longarm didn't know if they were all that was left of Roland's gunmen, but they had to represent the lion's share of the gang. Roland issued orders.

"Those other troublemakers are out there somewhere. Spread out and hunt them down. Kill them if you have to. But if you can, just disarm them and send them scurrying back to their holes like the craven mice they are. Cass, you're in charge of the hunt."

"What about you, Uncle Vance?"

The lantern-jawed undertaker pointed the gun in his hand at Longarm. "I'm not worried about Marshal Long. He's not going to try anything."

Cass didn't look so sure about that but he shrugged in acceptance of his uncle's orders. The outlaws filed out of the undertaking parlor, leaving Longarm and Vance Roland alone with the body of Arlo Snyder.

"Sit down, Marshal." Roland used the barrel of the gun to gesture at a ladderback chair adjacent to a coffin sitting on a pair of sawhorses.

Longarm picked up the chair, reversed it, and straddled it after moving it several feet away from the coffin. That brought a laugh from Roland.

"You don't want to be too close to your ultimate destination, eh? I'm not surprised. No one wants to think about death. Not even those of us who make it our profession."

Longarm knew he had to get out of here. Nicole and Tom Heath and the other townspeople from Antelope were out there in the blizzard, being stalked by killers. He had to do something to help them.

Roland was keeping his distance, though, being careful not to get close enough for Longarm to jump him and take that gun away. Longarm had to get him closer somehow. Maybe make him mad enough to stop being so cautious . . .

"How'd you go from being an honest businessman to running a gang of no-good, vicious, owlhoot skunks? Or were you ever a real undertaker?"

Roland bristled at the sneering tone of Longarm's voice. Just as the big lawman had hoped.

"Of course I was a real undertaker. It's an honorable profession."

"I never said it wasn't. I guess that's why you quit. No honor."

"I helped people in their time of need. And what did I get in return? My business failed because people wouldn't pay their bills. They wanted decent burials for their loved ones but they weren't willing to pay for them."

"That's what turned you crooked? You went out of business?" Longarm shook his head. He was still trying to goad Roland into coming closer, but he was also a mite amazed by what the ugly son of a bitch was telling him. "Plenty of folks go out of business without turning into desperadoes and murderers."

"They never realized what I did." Roland jabbed the Colt in his hand toward the coffin. "That's what's waiting for us all, don't you see, Marshal? You work and work and work . . . you suffer through all the miseries, big and small, that life has to hand out, and what sort of payoff is waiting for you at the end?" He laughed. "A pine box. That's what you get in return for all the suffering you go through. Once I realized that, I decided that if I was fated to be food for the worms anyway I might as well enjoy the trip getting there."

"So you became an owlhoot. You put a gang together and took over this town."

Roland finally took a step closer to Longarm. The deep-set eyes burned with a mad light in his ugly face.

"Have you ever known what it is to possess total power, Marshal? The power of life and death over people who might as well be ants to you? It's the most exhilarating feeling you can ever experience. That's why I told my men not to kill any more of those foolish townspeople than they have to. What pleasure is there in ruling a place with an iron fist if there's no one in it to feel fear when you walk by?"

Longarm wasn't so sure now if Roland was really crazy as a loon or just pure evil. Either way, the bastard had to be stopped. His grip on this settlement had to be broken.

Longarm's hands rested on the top rung of the chair's ladderlike back. They tightened around the wood as his muscles tensed. Roland was almost close enough now. Another step and Longarm would be able to spring to his feet and swing the chair up. The legs would knock Roland's gun aside before the undertaker could fire.

That was the plan, anyway, but first Longarm had to lure Roland just a little closer.

"You'll hang for what you've done, Roland. I'll see to that. You'll get your pine box payoff, all right. A cheap owlhoot's coffin and an unmarked grave in potter's field."

Roland's face got even uglier as an arrogant sneer formed on it. "That's big talk for a man who's unarmed, wounded, and helpless. Maybe I'll put a bullet in one of your knees. That won't kill you, but you'll be in agony from it." The undertaker took that last step Longarm needed. "To go along with the agony you'll feel as you're forced to watch what happens to that pretty young woman who was with you."

Longarm started up fast, bringing the chair with him as he rose.

But before he could strike a blow, the door burst open behind him. Wind gusted in, bringing with it swirls of snow and a shouted command.

"Hold it, Marshal!"

Cass Roland stepped into the room. The gun in his right hand pointed straight at Longarm's back.

Cass's left hand shoved a pale, frightened-looking Nicole Gardner in front of him. The outlaw's beard-stubbled face split in a savage grin.

"Look what I found, Uncle Vance!"

Chapter 24

Nicole stumbled a little, then caught her balance. From the look on her face Longarm thought for a second that she was going to turn around and attack Cass even though he had a gun in his hand. Then she controlled herself with visible effort and settled for sending a dark, murderous glare Cass's way.

"You showed up just at the right time, Cass." Roland's ugly face wore a smirk as he spoke. "Marshal Long here was about to get feisty."

"Yeah, I saw that." Cass motioned with the gun. "Sit down, Long. Try anything again and I'll blow a hole right through you."

Longarm settled back down onto the chair. He glared at Cass like Nicole was doing.

But of course it didn't do any good.

Nothing would in this situation except a gun in his hand spitting hot lead.

"Where did you find her?"

"Down the street next to the old saddle shop."

"What about Heath? Any sign of the good doctor?"

Longarm was a little surprised that Cass shook his head. "He wasn't anywhere around."

Longarm was curious. He would have figured that Heath would stay close to Nicole. But he couldn't very well ask her about it, not with Roland and Cass standing right there.

If Heath was still loose, that meant he might be able to come to their aid. In a situation as dire as this, every potential ally was a valuable one.

Longarm could tell that by now Nicole had noticed Snyder's body. She made a point of not looking at the bloody corpse. She was smart enough to figure out what had happened.

"We were betrayed."

Roland cackled with laughter. "Indeed you were, my dear. Arlo couldn't talk fast enough when he was threatened with death. Unfortunately for him it caught up to him anyway. I think you'll find that most people are like that when the chips are down. Cowards, through and through." A cunning look came into the undertaker's eyes. "You strike me as being different. We could torture you and it wouldn't do a bit of good. You'd spit in your tormentor's eye with your dying breath."

"Damn right I would."

"And I have a feeling that Marshal Long is the same way."

Longarm grinned from the chair. "You'll never find out, old son, because I don't plan on dying anytime soon."

Cass had gotten a worried look on his face. "Uncle Vance, I thing we oughta just go ahead and shoot both of 'em. They're tricky. Best not to take a chance on them trying anything."

Longarm could tell from Roland's expression that the undertaker was giving the suggestion some serious consideration. Longarm's muscles tensed again. If Roland and Cass opened fire, he would at least try to jump one of them. He was damned if he was going to die sitting placidly in a chair.

A sudden burst of shots outside from somewhere nearby made the two killers forget about Longarm and Nicole for the moment. Roland stepped back well out of reach and snapped an order to his nephew.

"Go see what that's about."

Cass nodded. "Some of the boys probably cornered another o' those damn townies." He opened the door, letting in another draft of cold, snowy air, then slammed it behind him as he left the undertaking parlor.

Roland grinned at Longarm and Nicole. "You two are lucky. You have a reprieve. I'm afraid Cass is right, though. When he gets back, we'll have to go ahead and kill you."

Longarm understood why Roland wanted to wait to carry out the murders. Nicole had edged away so that she and Longarm were separated by several feet. Roland had his gun pointed somewhere between them. If he turned to shoot one of them, the other would have a chance to jump him. That would be a risky move but better than having no chance at all. Roland wanted to wait for Cass to return so that Longarm and Nicole could die at the same time.

Longarm didn't intend to give Roland that luxury. He was going to force the undertaker to make a decision. His plan was to lunge out of the chair and leap at Roland. He'd probably die, but at least Nicole might be able to get her hands on the undertaker's gun that way.

"Hey, mister!"

The high-pitched voice came from behind Roland. None of them had noticed the small figure that had slipped into the open doorway between the undertaking parlor's front room and the rest of the building. Roland whirled around, swung the gun toward Jamey, who stood there with his right arm cocked back.

Jamey's arm flashed forward. Longarm leaped up and raised the chair at the same time. The snowball that Jamey had thrown struck Roland in the face and burst apart, blinding him. The gun in his hand roared, but it hadn't come in line with the boy's body yet. The bullet missed Jamey and thudded into the wall instead.

The next second the chair in Longarm's hands came crashing down over Roland's head. The chair shattered into pieces. Roland's skull was harder than that. But the blow was enough to knock him off his feet and make him drop the gun. He collapsed onto the floor, stunned.

Nicole rushed in and scooped the pistol from the floor. Longarm still had hold of a chair leg so he walloped Roland with it again. The undertaker wouldn't be regaining consciousness anytime soon.

Longarm took the pistol from Nicole and pushed her toward the door where Jamey had snuck in. "Out the back!" The snapped command was directed at both of them. "Jamey, where's the doc?"

"He's waitin' out there."

Nicole looked surprised. "He sent you in here to risk your life that way?"

"Naw, he didn't know about it. I snuck off and done it on my own."

"Enough talk." Longarm herded them toward the door. "Get moving. Find a place to lie low."

Nicole glanced back over her shoulder at him. "Custis, what are you going to do?"

"Cass probably heard that shot. He'll come a-running to make sure nothing happened to his uncle. I'll be waiting for him."

Nicole looked like she wanted to argue about leaving Longarm on his own. But Jamey tugged on her sleeve, urging her to the door. "Come on, ma'am. We'll go find Doc Heath."

Longarm nodded. That was exactly what he wanted Nicole to do. She had gotten separated from Heath somehow once and ended up getting herself captured. He didn't want that to happen again.

With one last look of mingled despair and hope, Nicole fled from the undertaking parlor. Longarm shut the door behind them. Then he blew out the single lamp that was burning in the room and waited for Cass Roland to return.

He didn't have to wait for long. Heavy footsteps sounded on the boardwalk just outside. Boldly, recklessly, Cass threw the front door open and rushed into the darkened room. He shouted, "Uncle Vance! Where are you?"

Longarm moved in behind him and clubbed at his head with the gun. Something, some wild animal's cunning and instinct, must have warned Cass. He twisted aside just as the blow fell. The gun cracked down on his shoulder instead. He howled in pain and his gun went off almost in Longarm's face. The roar was deafening and the flash practically seared the lawman's eyes. Longarm struck again but this blow was a blind one. He and Cass grappled in the darkness.

The two men staggered across the room, slammed into the wall. They bounced off and wheeled around. Longarm tripped on something. It was the door sill, he realized a second later when he found himself outside again. He and Cass had stumbled through the door and onto the boardwalk. Each man had hold of the wrist of the other's gun hand and were choking each other as well. With strangled grunts of effort they heaved at each other, trying to seize the advantage.

Suddenly nothing was under Longarm's feet except empty air. He felt himself falling but didn't let go of Cass.

The two men didn't fall very far. They had reached the edge of the boardwalk and plunged off into the street. Both men sprawled in the snow, which cushioned their landing and kept their grips from being knocked loose by the impact. As they rolled over, Cass drove a knee toward Longarm's groin but missed, hitting him on the thigh instead. It still hurt. Red rage flared inside Longarm. Feeling Cass's breath on his face, he lowered his head and thrust it forward as hard as he could, hunching his shoulders to put more power into the move.

Longarm heard a distinct *pop!* as his forehead flattened Cass's nose. Cass screeched. He lost his hold on Longarm's gun hand. Longarm smashed the revolver across Cass's face and did even more damage. He tightened his grip on Cass's neck, raised the gun and reversed, and brought the butt down again and again. It hit with a sound like a finger thumping a melon. Cass bucked a couple of times and then went still.

Longarm pushed himself up. His pulse hammered in his head, and he was both breathless from the struggle and a little sick at the brutality of his own actions. He had been fighting for his life, though, and didn't regret what he'd done. In the faint light from the buildings he made out Cass's body lying in the snow, but couldn't see how much damage he had done to the outlaw's face. He saw dark splashes in the snow around Cass's head that had to be blood. Heard the rasping, bubbling breaths that the man took.

Heard the way those breaths stopped, followed by a ghastly rattle in Cass's throat.

Longarm staggered to his feet. Cass was dead but the danger was far from over.

That was proven a second later when guns roared behind him.

Chapter 25

Longarm threw himself forward as bullets whistled past his head. He twisted as he fell so that when he landed in the snow he was facing toward the gunmen.

"He's down! The bastard's down! I hit him!"

Two of them. These varmints seemed to travel in pairs most of the time. They charged forward, thinking they'd blown holes in him.

Longarm let them come. He wanted them close. He didn't know how many bullets were left in the gun he had taken away from Vance Roland.

The wind wasn't any worse but the snow seemed to be coming down thicker than ever. Longarm couldn't see as far as he'd been able to earlier. The two killers were almost on top of him before he rose up and shot them, one . . . two. Both men doubled over screaming as Longarm's slugs tore into their bellies.

Longarm kicked their guns out of their hands as they writhed in the snow and stained the white, powdery stuff with their blood. One man grew still and then the other. Gut-shot like that they wouldn't be dead yet but they'd likely never regain consciousness, either. Longarm holstered his gun and picked up the weapons he'd kicked aside.

He heard movement behind him and spun, irons in both hands. The figure coming toward him thrust its arms out. "Custis! Don't shoot! It's me!"

Nicole.

Longarm dragged in a deep breath. The muscles in his forearms trembled a little from the effort he had put forth not to squeeze the triggers. The trembling eased as he lowered the guns. The cold air cleared his head.

"Damn it, gal, I almost ventilated you!"

Nicole stumbled up to him and clutched his arm. "I'm sorry, Custis. I thought that was you I saw and I didn't want us to get separated again." She tugged on him. "This way!"

She seemed to know where she was going so he let her lead the way. They crossed the street. A dark shape loomed up in front of them: the late Arlo Snyder's livery barn. The wind was cut off suddenly as they went inside. Someone swung the door shut behind them.

"You found him. You found the marshal." The boyish voice belonged to Jamey. "Want me to light the lantern?"

"Custis, do you think we can risk a light?"

Longarm thought it would be all right. "With the barn door closed and the snow coming down so thick, nobody will be able to see a little light coming through the cracks around the door. Just keep it turned low. You got a match, son?"

"Yeah. Just a minute."

Longarm heard the scrape of a match and saw it flare to life. Jamey held the flame to the wick of a lantern hanging on a peg driven into one of the thick posts supporting the hayloft. The wick caught. Jamey lowered the chimney and the lantern cast a small circle of yellow light.

Longarm looked around. He and Nicole and Jamey were the only humans in the barn. A few stalls held horses. Longarm had thought that Dr. Heath might be with them.

"Are you two all right?" Longarm asked.

"We're fine, Custis. Better now that you're here."

"Where's the doc?"

Nicole's voice was tight with worry and strain. "I don't know. We haven't seen him."

"How'd you get split up earlier?"

"Well, when it became obvious that you weren't going to be able to set the hardware store on fire like you were supposed to, I wanted to go see what was wrong. Thomas wouldn't let me. He was afraid you'd walked into a trap."

Longarm nodded. "That's what happened, all right. Roland and his bunch got their hands on Snyder. He told them what we planned to do. They were laying in wait for me in the hardware store."

"Thomas said it had to be something like that. Then Roland's men fanned out and started searching the town. We tried to get away but they spotted us. When they opened fire, Thomas made me go one way while he went the other. He turned back right toward those killers to draw their fire so that I'd have a chance to escape. I . . . I haven't seen him since then. They probably killed him." Her voice broke. "But his sacrifice was all for nothing because Cass and one of the others caught me a few minutes later anyway."

Jamey spoke up. "The doc wasn't dead when I saw him after that, Miss Nicole. Remember? I ran into him while he was sneakin' around to the back of the undertakin' parlor. That's when I slipped in there and threw that snowball at mean ol' Mr. Roland."

"But Heath was gone when the two of you went out the back?" Longarm asked.

"We didn't see him anywhere . . . but the snow was so thick by then . . ."

Longarm put a hand on Nicole's shoulder and squeezed. "Yeah, you could walk right past a fella a dozen feet away and maybe not see him in this blizzard. But don't give up on the doc. He could still be out there somewhere, doing just fine. He's probably looking for us right about now."

Nicole nodded. She put what was likely supposed to be a hopeful smile on her face.

"What about all the other men, the ones who were supposed to attack Roland's gunnies when the fire lured them out?"

"I have no idea. We haven't seen any of them. I heard some shots, though . . . I'm afraid Roland's men may have killed some of them."

Longarm had to admit that grim possibility might be true. The townsmen who had escaped the deadly search were probably lying low by now and would stay where they were unless they were discovered. Longarm's mouth was filled with a bitter taste. His plan would have worked if Arlo Snyder hadn't spilled his guts to Roland. Now things were all shot to hell.

"What are we going to do, Custis?"

Longarm nodded toward the stalls. "You could saddle up a couple of those horses, and you and the boy could ride out of here."

"Into that storm? We'd be lost and freeze to death before morning. Besides, what about you?"

Longarm set one of the pistols on a stool, began punching cartridges out of the cylinder of the other. "I figure on staying."

"You mean you're going to keep fighting."

"Somebody's got to." Longarm set aside the gun he had emptied. He thumbed some of the shells he had taken from it into the empty chambers of the other pistol. He reloaded the gun he had taken from Roland with the bullets he had left over. He felt Nicole's eyes on him but didn't let that distract him from his task. When he was finished, he had two fully loaded revolvers and a couple of extra bullets, which he slipped into one of the pockets in the sheepskin coat.

"Give me one of those guns."

He looked up at her, saw the determination in her eyes.

"I'm not running out on you, Custis. I've spent my whole life running before trouble could catch up to me. I'm tired of it. I want to stay and fight for a change." She gave a hollow laugh. "Not that I have much real choice in the matter—not with that blizzard raging outside."

"Oh, I reckon you've got a choice, all right." Longarm handed her one of the revolvers. "Everybody's got choices. Most folks live the way they do because deep down that's the way they want it. If it wasn't, they could just walk away from it."

"Or run away like I always did." She moved closer to him, rested her head against his chest as he lifted his arms and put them around her.

Jamey made a disgusted noise. "If you two are gonna get all mushy, I'm gonna go keep an eye out the door. There's a knothole I can look through."

"You do that, old son."

Longarm enjoyed holding Nicole. For one thing, it was warmer huddled together like that. He had no illusions about how things were going to turn out. Likely both of them would die here in Antelope. Even though he'd managed to kill some of Roland's men, the outlaws still outnumbered them by a considerable amount. And he and Nicole were probably on their own now. They couldn't count on any more help from the townspeople, not after the plan he'd worked out had been ruined.

And even if they survived somehow, there was still the matter of the charges against Nicole. Longarm believed her story about Miles Ambrose murdering Harvey Kellogg back in Virginia City. That version fit the facts he had observed just as well as the idea that Nicole had killed Kellogg. A little digging would uncover the truth there. Longarm had the feeling Miles Ambrose wouldn't stand up to much pressure.

But Nicole was wanted for other crimes and there was no doubt that she had committed them. She hadn't even denied them during the time Longarm had known her. Admittedly that hadn't been very long, but still . . .

So on one side he had his job and the responsibility he felt toward Billy Vail and toward the badge he carried, and on the other he had the fact that he and Nicole had made love, had fought side by side. And she had saved his life when she could have ridden off and left him to die.

Longarm didn't like moral dilemmas. Sure, he had bent the rules a mite a time or two during his career. More than a time or two, come to think of it. But like he had told Nicole, everybody faced choices and every choice a person made carried a price with it. A price that had to be paid and had to be lived with from that moment on.

He bent down, kissed the top of her head, and told himself not to worry so about it. First they had to live through the rest of this long, violent night . . .

Jamey's voice came from the doors of the stable where he had his eye pressed to the knothole he'd mentioned. "Somebody's comin' up the street. I think it's that mean ol' Mr. Roland. And he's got somebody with him . . . Holy jeepers! It's Doc Heath!"

Chapter 26

Longarm and Nicole rushed to the doors of the stable. Jamey stepped aside so that Longarm could lean over and press his eye to the knothole. Sure enough, he saw Vance Roland prodding Dr. Thomas Heath along in front of him. Every couple of steps Roland jabbed the barrels of his shotgun into Heath's back.

They stopped in the middle of the street. Roland raised his voice in a shout to compete with the howling of the frigid wind.

"Marshal Long! You hear me, Marshal Long?"

Longarm didn't answer. He waited to see what the undertaker was going to do. Beside him Nicole made small, worried noises.

"I've got Dr. Heath here, Marshal! My shotgun's pressed against his back and my thumb is the only thing holding back the hammers. If you shoot me, I'll let them go. And you know what will happen then!"

Longarm knew, all right: The double charge of buckshot would blow a huge hole through Heath. Pretty much blow him in half, in fact.

"I know you're out there, Marshal! I know you hear me! I can feel it! And you know I mean what I say! You and the woman come out with your hands up! Surrender or I'll kill the doctor!"

Nicole leaned closer to Longarm. "What are we going to do, Custis?" The strain she was under made her voice shake a little.

Longarm's face was set in grim, weary lines. "I reckon he means it. He'll kill the doc. But as soon as Roland lets go of those hammers, he's lost his bargaining chip. He won't be able to get back to cover before I blast some holes in him."

"But Thomas will still be dead."

"Yeah. There's that to consider."

Longarm had noticed that Nicole had started referring to Heath by his first name most of the time. Even though she had known the doctor for only a few hours, it seemed that she had already come to like him. That didn't bother Longarm. His instincts told him that Heath was a good man, despite the disfiguring injuries and the torture the sawbones had inflicted on himself because of the mine tragedy. And even though Longarm and Nicole had enjoyed some time together, neither had any sort of claim on the other.

At the moment the only bearing any of this had on the situation was whether or not Nicole would be tempted to do something foolish because of her newfound feelings for Tom Heath. Longarm knew they couldn't surrender. If they did, Roland would likely just go ahead and kill all of them, Heath included. But Nicole might not realize that.

Out in the street Roland was growing impatient. "Long! You better answer me, mister! My thumb's getting tired of holding these hammers back!"

Nicole squeezed Longarm's shoulder. "Custis . . ."

Longarm straightened from the knothole and turned to Jamey. "I reckon this place has got a back door?"

"Sure."

"Take Miss Nicole and go out that way."

Nicole shook her head. "I told you, Custis, I'm not running anymore."

"I ain't asking you to run. You're gonna circle around and get behind Roland. Be careful, though. Stay behind cover as much as you can. I'd bet a hat he's got some of his gunnies holed up over there in the undertaking parlor with rifles trained on the street."

"You're going to try to get Thomas away from him without surrendering?"

Longarm nodded. "That's the plan." He didn't know if it would work or not, but he supposed at this point any plan was better than none.

"All right. Give me a couple of minutes." She stepped closer to him and gave him an impulsive kiss.

One way or another it was good-bye, Longarm sensed.

Jamey made a face. "Are we goin' or not?"

Longarm grinned at the boy. "You keep your head down, partner, you hear?"

"Sure, sure. Come on, ma'am."

With a last look at Longarm, Nicole let Jamey lead her into the shadows at the rear of the cavernous barn. They disappeared into the gloom.

"By God, Marshal, I'm going to count to ten! If you're not out here by then, you can watch me blow the good doctor in half!"

Longarm grimaced. He would have preferred giving Nicole more time to get into position, but Roland wasn't going to allow them that luxury.

"One . . . two . . ."

Longarm listened to the undertaker's raspy voice as Roland counted off the remaining seconds of Dr. Thomas Heath's life. He delayed as long as he dared. But when Roland reached "eight" Longarm swung one of the stable doors open and stepped out into the wind-driven snow.

"Roland! I'm here!"

The undertaker grabbed the collar of Heath's duster

with his free hand and swung the doctor around, keeping the shotgun against his back at the same time. Roland stopped so that Heath formed an effective shield between him and Longarm. Longarm walked slowly toward them. His arm was extended out in front of him with the gun in his hand leveled.

Roland spoke when Longarm was about twenty feet away. "That's close enough, Marshal! Now drop your gun or I'll kill the doctor!"

Longarm shook his head. "What proof do I have that hombre actually *is* the sawbones? In that duster and hood he could be anybody. Could even be one of your men."

"You want proof?" Roland laughed. His free hand went to the hood on Heath's head. "I'll give you proof! Look upon the monster and know the truth!"

He ripped the hood off, revealing Tom Heath's hideously scarred visage. Heath shook with rage and humiliation. His eyes, the only thing still normal about him, flared in his ruined face. Longarm saw that and knew that Roland had just pushed Heath too far. Heath started to twist around, turning with desperate speed in an attempt to get his body away from the barrels of that shotgun.

Flame bloomed from the Greener. Heath was flung aside by the buckshot that slammed into him. Longarm fired at the same time. Roland was already jerking aside, though, so Longarm's bullet missed him, sizzling past bare inches away from the undertaker's head.

"No!"

That cry came from Nicole, who charged along the street from the other direction. The gun in her hand spouted flame. Roland dashed through the snow, headed back toward the undertaking parlor. Longarm snapped another shot at him. Roland stumbled, hit by either Longarm or Nicole, but kept going.

Heath struggled to get to his feet. Longarm ran to his side, bent to get his free arm under one of Heath's arms. As he lifted the doctor, more shots began to ring out as Roland's men opened fire.

"Nicole! Get back!" Longarm waved his gun toward her, motioning her away from the storm of lead that had suddenly erupted in the street. Longarm swung around toward the livery barn. From the corner of his eye he saw Roland bound on to the boardwalk and then race inside the building. As fast as he was moving, he couldn't have been wounded very badly.

Bullets whipped around Longarm and Heath and kicked up snow around their feet as Longarm hustled the doctor toward the stable. Heath stumbled along, mostly dead weight but able to help a little. Slugs thudded into the walls of the barn as Longarm and Heath practically fell through the door that Longarm had left open when he came out.

As he lay on the ground next to Heath, Longarm kicked the door shut. That would give them a respite, if only momentarily. Roland would probably order his men to storm the barn now that he knew Longarm and Heath were inside.

Longarm pushed himself to his feet and reached back down to help Heath up. "Come on, Doc. We can't stay here. We've got to keep moving."

Heath groaned as he struggled upright with Longarm's assistance.

"How bad are you hit?"

"Some of the pellets . . . got me in the side." Heath's voice was thick with pain. "Hurts like hell . . . but not as bad . . . as it might've been."

Longarm nodded as he helped Heath toward the rear of the stable. "You were close enough to that scattergun so that the charges didn't have time to spread out much. That's why you were able to duck away from them. Roland might've had better luck killing you if he'd backed off a mite."

A grim chuckle came from Heath. "It's a good thing . . . he was too anxious, then."

"Yeah." Longarm found the rear door and shouldered through it. He and the doctor stumbled back out into the storm. He wasn't sure where to go now, but like he had told Heath, they had to keep moving. That was their only chance. He wanted to find Nicole again if they could. Might be hard to do in this blizzard, though.

Longarm and Heath trudged through the snow, bent over against the wind. Longarm was chilled to the bone and knew that Heath probably was, too.

But that was likely a good thing because he would be too cold to really feel the pain from the wounds in his side. Chances were the doc was numb enough from the cold that those buckshot wounds weren't bothering him too much. If they ever got warm again, both of them would probably hurt like blazes.

But that was a mighty big "if."

A figure suddenly loomed in front of them in the wind-blown whiteness. Longarm stopped and swung his gun up. Held off on the trigger as he heard Jamey's voice.

"Marshal! Marshal, is that you? Where's Doc Heath?"

"Right here with me, Jamey." Longarm lowered the revolver. "Give me a hand with him. He's been hurt."

"Yeah, I saw what happened. I was hidin' in a wagon down the street from where you had that shoot-out with Mr. Roland." Jamey moved up on Heath's other side and got an arm around the doctor's waist. "You can lean on me some, Doc. I may be little but I'm pretty strong."

They started moving through the blizzard again. "You know some place you can hide the doc for a little while, Jamey?"

"There's a cave in the creek bank not far from here. It'd be out of the wind anyway. And Mr. Roland's men might not know to look there."

"Can you find it in this storm?"

"Sure. I know my way around, even with a little snow fallin'."

Longarm hoped the boy's confidence wasn't misplaced. There was a lot more than a "little" snow falling. But Heath was in no shape to do any more fighting so they had to find a place where he could hole up for a while.

"Can you get him there by yourself?"

"I reckon."

"Ever use a gun?"

"Sure!"

Longarm took the extra pistol from behind his belt and gave it to Jamey as Heath leaned against a tree trunk for a moment and rested. "Don't use it unless you have to. And if you do, make sure whoever you shoot at is Roland or one of his men."

"I understand, Marshal. I won't let you down."

"No, I don't reckon you will."

"My hood. I need my hood." Heath sounded only half-coherent.

"You're fine without it for now, Doc. Nobody cares what you look like."

Heath muttered something but didn't really argue. Longarm asked Jamey the other question he needed answered.

"What about Miss Nicole? Did you see what happened to her?"

"Yeah." Jamey's voice caught a little. "Mr. Roland sent his men out again, right after he ran back into the undertakin' parlor. I think . . . I think some of them grabbed Miss Nicole. I heard her scream."

Longarm's jaw tightened. If Jamey was right, then Roland had himself another hostage. Longarm had to get back to the settlement and reach the undertaking parlor somehow, even though Roland's gunmen were probably spread out all around it. Roland was bound to know that Longarm would come for Nicole.

As Jamey and Heath stumbled off toward the cave that would be their hideout for a while, Longarm took the extra rounds from his coat pocket and reloaded the Colt. As he thumbed in the cartridges, a grim look came over his face.

It was time to end this.

One way or the other.

Chapter 27

Longarm struggled up out of the darkness that engulfed him. The first thing he noticed was that he wasn't cold anymore. In fact, he was downright hot. Waves of heat pounded against him.

The explanation was simple: He had died and gone to hell. His sins had caught up with him at last.

He even heard the Devil laughing.

"Good job, Forrest. You laid out the marshal just fine."

No, not the Devil. Both the laugh and the voice belonged to Vance Roland.

Same thing, more or less.

Longarm didn't open his eyes. Didn't budge or give any other sign that he had regained consciousness. But even though his body was still, his mind was in motion. Racing, in fact, as memories came flooding back in on his brain.

He remembered making his way back into Antelope after leaving Dr. Heath and Jamey. Remembered how the storm had intensified until he could barely see his hand in front of his face and the wind nearly blew him off his feet. He recalled as well the gunfights, and crawling under that porch, and taking the shotgun away from the man he had knocked out. Mixed in with those scenes as they played

*themselves over in his head were the screams, which came
from Nicole. Longarm saw again how he had burst into the
undertaking parlor, blasted another of Roland's gunnies
with the shotgun, then . . .*

Then somebody had walloped him from behind, knock-
ing him out. He sensed now that he hadn't been unconscious for very long. No more than a minute or two, more
than likely. But that was long enough for him to have been
disarmed. He cracked one eye open the barest fraction of
an inch. That was enough to show him the legs of the cast-
iron stove with their clawlike feet. He'd been dragged
across the room and dumped beside the stove. That's why
he was so hot. He figured steam must be rising from the
melted snow that had covered his clothes when he came in.

He was also next to the coffin that had been knocked off
the sawhorses earlier. The body of the man he'd blasted
with the shotgun was gone, probably dragged outside, but
the debris from the busted-up coffin remained.

"Want me to go ahead and shoot the son of a bitch, Mr.
Roland?"

The question probably came from the man who had hit
Longarm from behind. Still without betraying that he was
awake, Longarm waited for Roland's answer.

"No, there's no longer any need to rush. With Marshal
Long and the woman as our prisoners we don't have to
worry about Dr. Heath. He won't try anything, even if he's
still alive. And he may not be since I clipped him pretty
good with that shotgun blast."

"What about the rest of those townies who were bent on
causin' trouble?"

Roland's laugh was full of disdain. "I'd wager they're
all cowering in their beds by now, hoping that no one will
come for them in the night. Without Long to lead them
they're harmless."

Longarm hoped that wasn't the case but worried that it
was. The citizens of Antelope had allowed Roland and his

gang to come in and take over. They had been reluctant to stand up for themselves. And once the planned attack had fallen through, they had disappeared in a hurry, leaving Longarm, Nicole, Dr. Heath, and Jamey to carry on the fight against the outlaws. A lady con artist, a disfigured and emotionally crippled doctor, and a little boy—that wasn't much of an army.

"What do you want me to do, boss?"

"Go find all the boys who are left and bring them back here. The trouble's over for tonight. Come morning we'll give these yokels a lesson they'll never forget. I intend to hang Marshal Long up in the street and strip the hide off him while he's still alive. Then we'll leave the bloody carcass hanging there as a reminder of what will happen to anyone who dares to challenge me."

"What about the girl?" Longarm could almost see the lustful expression on the outlaw's face as he asked the question.

"You and the rest of the men can have her. I won't have any use for her."

"She's mighty pretty, boss."

"Women don't interest me. Power does."

Yeah, Roland was one sick son of a bitch. But he might get away with what he planned to do unless Longarm could figure out some way of turning the tables on him. He would bide his time, pretend to still be out cold until the other outlaw was gone and Roland was alone again . . .

"Oh, by the way. Before you go, take your knife and cut Marshal Long's hamstrings. Just to be sure that he doesn't get any funny ideas when he regains consciousness."

Longarm's teeth ground together. Roland was unwittingly forcing his hand. He would have to make a try at jumping the other outlaw and getting his gun before the hombre crippled him.

Before that could happen, the door of the undertaking parlor burst open again. "Boss!" It was a new voice. "They're comin'!"

Longarm opened his eyes and lifted his head as footsteps rushed across the floor. He saw Roland and the other
outlaw with their backs now turned toward him while a
third owlhoot stood just inside the door with the wind
whipping snow around him.

"Who's coming, you damned fool?"

Longarm's gaze flicked to Nicole, who stood against the
other wall with her arms behind her. He could tell from her
unnatural position that her hands were tied behind her. Her
eyes widened with surprise when she saw that he was awake.

"It's the t-townies! The whole l-lot of 'em! They got
g-guns!" The newcomer was so excited he had to force the
words out.

"By God, I never would have believed they had the guts
to defy me again!"

"It's that d-doc! The one whose face got burned off!
He's leadin' 'em!"

"Damn it! I should have made sure he was dead when I
had the chance. Well, I won't make the same mistake
twice." Roland started to turn. "Kill Long and the girl . . ."

While they were talking, Longarm had been forcing
sore, stiff muscles to work. Every nerve in his body
screamed in protest, but he forced himself to his feet anyway. As he surged upright, he snatched one of the broken
pieces of coffin off the floor. He held it in front of him like
a lance as he yelled and threw himself across the room. He
aimed the jagged end of the board at Roland.

The startled undertaker was quick enough to jump behind the man who had clouted Longarm from behind.
That man screamed as the sharp, broken board drove into
his belly. Longarm kept moving, kept his legs churning.
Rammed the jagged board deep into the outlaw's guts and
forced him backward. The man crashed into Roland and
the owlhoot who had just run in with the warning. All four
men staggered across the boardwalk and plunged into the
street.

Longarm was instantly surrounded by the cold white hell of the blizzard again. He lost his footing, fell to the ground, rolled over, and got his mouth and nose full of snow. Sputtering, he scrambled upright again. He was aware now that gunfire was erupting somewhere nearby. He saw muzzle flashes all around. War had come to Antelope: war between the surviving outlaws from Roland's gang and the townspeople who had been aroused to action again by Dr. Thomas Heath. Longarm had thought that the sawbones was too badly wounded for something like that, but obviously Heath had found the strength somewhere. There would have been no mistaking his disfigured face.

The man Longarm had rammed with the broken board lay nearby. The board stuck straight up from his belly, which was awash with blood. Longarm bent and snagged the gun from the holster on the dying man's hip.

He armed himself just in time because a second later Colt flame bloomed to his right and he heard the wind-rip of a slug beside his ear. Twisting, he brought the gun up and saw the outlaw who had brought the warning to the undertaking parlor. Longarm dropped to a knee and fired twice as fire spouted again from the muzzle of the man's gun.

That shot missed, too, but both of Longarm's bullets caught the owlhoot in the chest and knocked him backward, lifting him off his feet at the same time. He crashed down on his back in the snow and landed in the sort of limp sprawl that signified death.

"You damned meddler! Why won't you just *die*?"

The hate-filled scream came from Vance Roland. The undertaker was behind Longarm. As he tried to turn, Longarm knew he was going to be too late. The gun in Roland's shaking hand was ready to blast him.

But then Roland flinched as a snowball pelted him. Just as Jamey had done earlier in the evening, Nicole had freed herself somehow and struck with the only weapon close at hand. She had scooped up a double handful of snow from the boardwalk in front of the undertaking parlor, packed it together, and heaved it at Roland's head. Her aim had been true and a smile broke across her face as she saw the snowball hit its target.

Longarm took all that in during the split second it took Roland to jerk his gun toward Nicole and pull the trigger. She cried out, staggered back, doubled over.

"Nicole!"

The roar came from Dr. Thomas Heath, who loomed up out of the storm with a rifle in his hands. He still wasn't wearing his hood and his face was like something out of a nightmare as fury further contorted the scarred visage. Roland whirled toward him, then seemed to remember Longarm. For a second the undertaker's head snapped back and forth as he tried to figure out what to do.

Then his head exploded and his ugly face disappeared in a spray of blood as Longarm and Heath both opened fire at the same time. Roland was dead but his body was still upright, held there for a few seconds by the blizzard of lead the two men were pouring into it. Only when the guns fell silent did the bullet-shredded corpse collapse like a puppet with its strings cut.

Longarm got to his feet, swayed, and nearly fell. He caught himself on the broken board sticking up from the body of the man he had gored a few minutes earlier. Longarm ripped the coffin board loose, stumbled over to Roland, and buried the bloody, jagged end of it in the undertaker's body.

"There. There's your pine box payoff, you son of a bitch."

Heath rushed past him toward the undertaking parlor. Nicole was sprawled on the boardwalk in front of the building. Longarm turned and started after the doctor, nearly fell again. Somebody appeared beside him, caught hold of him, and helped him stay on his feet.

"Lemme give you a hand, Marshal."

Longarm looked down at Jamey and blinked bleary eyes. "Much obliged, partner. You all right?"

"Yeah, I'm fine. Sorry I couldn't make the doc stay in the cave like you told me to. When he got his breath back, he said he had to come help you and Miss Nicole."

Longarm limped toward the building, helped along by the youngster. "Got the townsfolk to fight back after all, did he?"

"Yeah. He went from house to house and said they had to help you. Told 'em it was time to stand up for theirselves and to stop lettin' other folks do their fightin' for them. I guess it worked. The shootin's over. I think our side won."

Longarm thought so, too. He looked around and saw other figures emerging from the swirling snow, converging on the undertaking parlor. Some of them he recognized from the meeting earlier, others he didn't, but all of them bore the stamp of small-town citizens instead of owlhoots and killers. Good solid folks . . . even if Tom Heath had been forced to shame them into fighting for what was right.

Longarm reached the boardwalk and leaned on one of the posts that supported the awning over it. Heath had sat down on the walk and lifted Nicole's head into his lap. His gloved, strangely gentle hands stroked the blonde hair back out of her face. "Miss Gardner." His voice was choked with emotion. "Nicole."

The blue eyes opened, peered up at him. "Thomas." His name was a weak whisper from her lips.

"Don't look at me."

"Don't be . . . silly. You're a very . . . handsome man." Without moving her head Nicole tried to look around. "Where's . . . Custis?"

Longarm leaned over her. "Right here, Nicole."

"I told you . . . I could throw a snowball."

"You sure did. Saved my life with it, too." He reached down, took hold of one of her hands, squeezed it.

Heath looked up at Longarm. "Help me get her inside."

Desperation drew his voice taut. "I've got to look at that wound. It may not be too late. Maybe I can still save her—"

"No, Doc. I'll help you carry her in, but it's too late to save her life."

"Damn you! Don't say that! It's not too late—"

Nicole sighed. Her eyes slipped closed and she lay still.

"I'm afraid it is, Doc." Longarm laid a hand on Heath's shoulder and squeezed hard. "But listen to me. There *is* still one thing you can do for her . . ."

Chapter 28

Longarm never knew her true name, so Nicole Gardner was what they put on the marker. He didn't know when she'd been born, either, so all they added to the name was the date of death. That would have to be enough.

With the wounds that both he and Thomas Heath had suffered, neither of them were in good enough shape to dig a grave. Several of the men from Antelope volunteered to take care of that. The next day after the battle, after the blizzard had moved on, under a bright and shining sun, they cleared away the snow from a space in the local cemetery and brought out the picks and shovels. The top of the ground was frozen, making it hard to dig, but the freeze didn't extend down very far. By working hard at it, the men had the grave ready by the middle of the day.

They brought a wagon to the undertaking parlor, drew the vehicle to a stop in front, and went inside the building. Longarm and Heath had the coffin ready. The townsmen lifted it, grunting a little under the weight. Then they carried it outside, placed it in the back of the wagon, and drove up the hill to the cemetery.

There would be other burials to take care of—Vance

Roland, his nephew Cass, the rest of the outlaws who had been wiped out in the fight during the snowstorm. Longarm didn't care about any of that. He just wanted to get Nicole's coffin in the ground so he could start back to Virginia City.

Quite a few people turned out for the service. Tom Heath stood at the head of the grave after the coffin had been lowered into it and he read from the Bible. He wasn't wearing his hood. He had taken to turning up the collar of his duster and pulling down the brim of his hat so that his scarred features were somewhat obscured but not completely concealed. He had told Longarm that he was tired of hiding his face from the world.

Longarm thought that was a fine idea and said as much to Heath. Anyway, once you got used to it, the doc didn't really look all that bad.

When the service was over and men were shoveling dirt into the grave, Heath climbed onto the wagon seat and reached down to give Jamey a hand. The boy scrambled up beside him.

Longarm had already swung up into the saddle. He rode over to the wagon and paused beside it.

"Where do you plan on going, Doc?"

Heath shook his head. "I don't really know. Away from here, at least for a while. Antelope has too many bad memories for me now. It might be better to start over somewhere." The thin-lipped mouth curved in a smile as he looked over at Jamey. "And I have a son to think of now. A family. I'm going to find a lawyer and start the process of legally adopting Jamey."

"Will I have to call you Pa instead of Doc, Doc?"

Heath chuckled at the youngster's question. "I think that would probably be a good idea."

Longarm held out a hand to Heath. "Good luck to you, Doctor."

"Thank you, Marshal." Heath still wore his gloves. One

178

step at a time. He gave Longarm's hand a firm grip. "Thank you for everything."

Longarm waved in farewell as Heath turned the wagon around and drove away. Jamey looked back and returned the wave with his typical enthusiasm.

Heath didn't look back. He had his eyes focused on the future.

So did Longarm. He swung his horse to the north and headed for Virginia City.

"I appreciate you seeing me like this, Mr. Ambrose." Longarm sat down in front of the desk in the office of the bank president and cocked his right ankle on his left knee. He slid a cheroot out of his vest pocket but didn't light it.

The bullet holes in his side still ached a mite, but they were healing just fine according to the local sawbones who had checked them. Nicole and then Tom Heath had done a good job of taking care of Longarm's wounds. There was a good chance he owed his life to them.

The slender, sandy-haired Ambrose smiled. "I'm glad to see you made it back safely, Marshal. Were you able to apprehend Miss Gardner?"

"She's dead." Longarm's voice was flat.

"Oh."

Ambrose looked surprised but not displeased. In fact he looked mighty pleased with himself, sitting in the bank president's office like this. He had been appointed to the position by the bank's board of directors, after Harvey Kellogg's death, since Ambrose knew more about the bank's operation than anyone else.

"Well, I suppose in its own way that justice has been carried out. Poor Mr. Kellogg's murder has been avenged."

Longarm's teeth clamped down hard on the unlit cheroot. "Not really."

Ambrose's eyebrows rose. "I don't understand. If the person responsible for his murder is dead—"

179

"That ain't the case."

Worry started to lurk in Ambrose's eyes behind the spectacles. "But if Miss Gardner is dead—"

Longarm interrupted him again. "She ain't the one who killed Kellogg." Longarm took the cheroot out of his mouth and laid it on the front edge of the desk. He put both feet on the floor and sat forward in the comfortable leather chair. "You are, Ambrose."

The man's eyes widened. He tried to look astounded but only succeeded in looking scared.

"My God, Marshal, how can you say such a thing? I saw her shoot him with my own eyes!"

A grim smile touched Longarm's mouth under the sweeping mustache. "Now, that ain't what you told me before, old son. You said the shots woke you up and when you came downstairs you found the gal standing over Kellogg with the gun in her hand."

"Well, of course that's what happened! I simply meant that the evidence I saw with my own eyes was incontrovertible. She killed him. She's the only one who could have."

"That ain't the way she told me the story."

"You talked to her before she died?" The fear in Ambrose's eyes was getting stronger.

"Yep. She said it was the other way around. Said she heard the shots and came in to find you with the gun in your hand."

Ambrose rocked his chair back angrily and made a curt gesture. "Of course she would lie about it! She was trying to save her own hide, after all. Honestly, I'm disappointed in you, Marshal. I didn't think you'd be taken in by such a blatant falsehood."

"Whether I believed her story or not I'd have to have proof."

Ambrose spread his hands. "It's her word against mine and since she's dead and I'm not . . ." He shrugged as if to say that the entire point was moot.

"She didn't have a reason to kill him. You did."

"That's insane. What reason would I have to murder poor Mr. Kellogg?"

"I reckon he must've found out that you'd been stealing from the bank right along."

A sharply indrawn breath hissed between Ambrose's teeth. "That's a lie!"

"We'll see." Longarm jerked his left thumb over his shoulder. "I wired Carson City and had the state bank examiners sent in. They're out there now going through the books. If there's anything to find, I reckon they'll find it. And they won't be leaving here until they do."

The way Ambrose's already pale face took on an even greater ashen pallor told Longarm that his guess was right. So did the way Ambrose's hand darted toward an open drawer in the desk.

"You son of a—"

He didn't get all the curse out of his mouth before Longarm's fist slammed into it. The big lawman had come up out of his seat as soon as Ambrose made his move. Ambrose's chair went over backward and he crashed to the floor, stunned. Blood welled from his smashed lips.

As Longarm leaned over the desk, he looked down into the drawer and saw the revolver Ambrose had tried to grab. "I reckon that's the final nail in your coffin, old son. I ain't as easy to kill as that old man was."

Longarm went around the desk, bent over, and grasped Ambrose's arm, hauling the murderer to his feet. Then he marched him out of the bank and straight to jail.

Longarm felt a twinge or two in his side, which he suspected came from the exertion of walloping Ambrose. It was a small price to pay for bringing a killer to justice and clearing the name of an innocent woman.

Well, sort of innocent, anyway.

With Ambrose locked up and the evidence gathered by the bank examiners forming a nice solid case against him,

Longarm went to the telegraph office to wire the results of the case to Billy Vail. Vail would have to break the news to the congressman that Nicole was dead. That closed the books on this assignment.

When he was done sending the telegram, Longarm stepped outside. The air was still chilly but the sun was shining and the snow had begun to melt . . . until the next storm that came along.

He took out a lucifer and set fire to the gasper he'd been chewing ever since leaving the bank. Now he drew in the smoke and blew it back out in a perfect ring. He hoped the passes to the south of Antelope had been clear enough for the wagon to get through. By now Tom Heath and Jamey ought to be a good long way from the settlement. . . .

With Nicole right beside them, the third member of their newly formed family. The disfigured doc, the orphaned kid, the shady lady . . . Hell, they belonged together. They all had a chance to start over and make something new and clean from their lives.

Longarm had seen right away when he reached the boardwalk in front of the undertaking parlor that Nicole wasn't badly wounded. Roland's bullet had barely scratched her, even though it must have hurt like blazes. Heath would have realized that, too, if he hadn't been so scared and upset. But Longarm had kept everybody out of the place after he and Heath carried her inside, so the citizens of Antelope truly believed that she was dead. If the question ever came up, that was the story they'd tell. The coffin that had been buried in the town cemetery with the simple marker had certainly felt heavy enough to contain a body. Longarm had piled enough rocks in it to make sure of that.

After Heath patched up Nicole's wound, Longarm had slipped her out of town before dawn. The blizzard had stopped. He was able to find a place to hide her, an old prospector's shack that Jamey had told him about. Heath and the boy had picked her up the next day after leaving the settlement.

The only ones who knew the truth were Longarm, Heath, Jamey . . . and Nicole herself. Longarm knew he might have a few uneasy moments in the future whenever he thought about the deception he had perpetrated. But he figured he could live with those misgivings easier than he could the feeling he'd have been left with if he'd sent her to prison. The way he saw it, she deserved a second chance.

That rock-filled coffin would give it to her. Nicole had gotten her own pine box payoff, a totally different sort from the one that had been waiting for Vance Roland . . .

Longarm grinned at that thought as he strolled away from the telegraph office under the clear blue Nevada sky.

Watch for

**LONGARM AND THE
TINY THIEF**

the 353rd novel in the exciting LONGARM
series from Jove

Coming in April!

GIANT-SIZED ADVENTURE FROM AVENGING ANGEL LONGARM.

BY TABOR EVANS

2006 GIANT EDITION

LONGARM AND THE OUTLAW EMPRESS
978-0-515-14235-8

2007 GIANT EDITION

LONGARM AND THE GOLDEN EAGLE SHOOT-OUT
978-0-515-14358-4

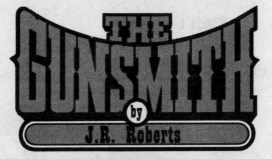

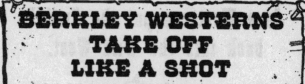